Disney
PETER PAN & WENDY

Tiger Lily and the *Secret Treasure* of *Neverland*

Cherie Dimaline

Disney PRESS
LOS ANGELES • NEW YORK

Published by Disney Press, an imprint of
Buena Vista Books, Inc. No part of this book may be
reproduced or transmitted in any form or by any means,
electronic or mechanical, including photocopying, recording, or
by any information storage and retrieval system, without written
permission from the publisher. For information address
Disney Press, 1200 Grand Central Avenue,
Glendale, California 91201.

Printed in the United States of America
First Hardcover Edition, March 2023
1 3 5 7 9 10 8 6 4 2
FAC-004510-23034

Library of Congress Control Number: 2022939324
ISBN 978-1-368-08046-0

Visit disneybooks.com

SUSTAINABLE FORESTRY INITIATIVE Certified Sourcing
www.sfiprogram.org
SFI-01681

Logo applies to Text Stock only

Foreword

Like the other characters in the *Peter Pan* tale, Tiger Lily is a fictional character who has lived in our imaginations for over a century. But unlike the other characters, Tiger Lily and her tribe are the original inhabitants of Neverland. So while Peter and the Lost Boys can trace their origins back to England and other points abroad, Tiger Lily is unique. She is the one main character who is from this land and who therefore has a deep connection with it. She is the ultimate narrator and the best guide to Neverland.

Since she is Native to this particular place, writing her story and creating her beautiful community was about finding the pieces of collective Indigenous philosophy and worldview (or as close to collective as possible) without borrowing too much from the existing and distinct Indigenous Nations across Turtle Island.

This book is not a story about Indigenous North Americans. Each Nation has their own stories and their own storytellers, and that is who should be heard and read if you are interested in Native American, Alaska Native, First Nations, Métis, and Inuit stories. This book is about Tiger Lily and her vibrant community and the ways she lives, protects, and loves her Neverland. Because Neverland has always been hers.

And so this book is dedicated to Tiger Lily, at last.

Chapter One

Tiger Lily watched as Peter Pan scrambled up a willow tree and, in a flash, began swinging upside down above her, with a giant tangle of vines shaped like a ball under his arm.

"Peter, that's out of bounds," Tiger Lily said, trying to be stern, but he looked so ridiculous with his hair all sticking up and his shirt drooping under his neck that she couldn't help smiling.

"That's out of bounds," Peter Pan said, mimicking her as he swung back and forth by his knees. They'd been playing another new game he'd brought back from his travels outside their home, Neverland. He had spent the morning trying to teach them the rules, but now

he kept changing them: first they couldn't use their hands; then they could; they weren't allowed to run, only skip; then they were supposed to run as fast as they could. It was hard to keep up.

"I'm serious! We specifically had to stay on the ground," Tiger Lily reminded him, though she laughed. She was laughing not at Peter in the tree but at the pile of Lost Boys struggling on the grass nearby. As they'd all dived for the vine-ball, they'd landed like this, their limbs all knotted together. Bundled up like that, they hadn't even noticed that Peter had the vine-ball now.

"Lily, look at me! Watch this!" Peter shouted. He had swung right side up and sat on the branch, balancing the vine-ball on his head and wobbling back and forth to keep it there.

"Do you not see this mess?" she responded, clutching her belly and pointing to the children in the field. "Someone should tell them the ball is gone."

"Yes, but watch me." Peter didn't like to be anything other than the center of attention. "I'm the best, most trickiest vine-baller in the land!"

Tiger Lily was used to Peter's antics. They had been friends since before she could remember. She sighed, rolled her eyes, and clapped for him as he bounced the vines off his head twice, his tongue sticking out of the corner of his mouth. "Very nice. Now, about these Boys . . ."

Curly, a pale girl wearing a bunny hat over her brown hair, was on the bottom, kicking and squirming. The identical twins, both with curly hair, brown skin, and the same flashing brown eyes, finished each other's sentences as they demanded the ball, each girl declaring sole ownership of it. And poor Nibs, a dirty seven-year-old boy wearing a fox costume, was stuck somewhere in the middle, trying desperately to hold his glasses on his face. It was probably a good thing the rest of the Lost Boys were off on a camping adventure, or this could have been a real mess.

"Come on, I only have the one pair," Nibs pleaded.

Suddenly, there was a buzzing across the field, like a swarm of bees, but wearing full armor, metallic and shrill. Tiger Lily focused, the way you are supposed to in order to truly listen, and words came through the harsh jingling: *"Lily! Come quick!"*

She turned and ducked just in time to avoid colliding with a very fast fairy, flying full speed at her.

"Sashi?" On her knees still, Tiger Lily called out, recognizing her best friend. "What is it? What's wrong?"

"Hey, Sashi, you wanna play? Try to catch me," called Peter. He jumped out of the tree and ran circles around her.

"Tiger Lily," Sashi gasped, chiming in her fairy language, which her friend had learned to understand long ago. Her curly hair was pulled back in tight braids, and her eyes were wide with fear. She paused, trying to catch enough breath to speak. "You have to go home, right now."

"She can't go home. We're in the middle of a game," Peter said, pouting and bouncing the ball on his knees between them. He seemed to understand her words, having a fairy best friend himself: Tinker Bell.

"There's a monster in the village!"

Sashi must be playing her own game now. A monster? In her quiet village? There was just no way. And yet from the look on her face and the fear in her voice, Tiger Lily knew the horrible truth: it was no game. She took off running before another word could be said.

Immediately, fear and confusion crowded Tiger Lily's head. Why hadn't she brought her horse, Pony? It would have been so much faster to get home on horseback. And how could there be a monster she didn't know of in Neverland? Was it one of the crocodiles from the swamp gone mad? Maybe a pirate come over to cause mischief wearing some sort of getup?

She flipped through all the possible scenarios in her mind until she noticed Peter Pan and Sashi taking the lead, rushing ahead of her, straight for the village: the place where she had been born and had always lived, and where everyone in her family was right then, in grave danger.

The Lost Boys had untangled themselves and were trying to catch up to her, letting out their best scary yells, promising to kill whatever beast threatened their friends.

"We'll stop that . . ."

"Thing in its tracks!" The twins finished one threat between them. Bits of grass and leaves stuck in their wild curls from rolling on the ground. They were identical down to their voices, except one wore a red coat over her white dress and the other wore a blue one so people could tell them apart.

"Wait up. You'll need reinforcements," Curly shouted, practical even in her fury.

Tiger Lily took to the forest with ease, moving swiftly through the trees and jumping over roots and rocks without looking. Bursting out the other side, she heard the screams just as the smoke from the cooking fires came into view.

Her parents, all her cousins—everyone was there. Everyone except for the hunters under the command of her great-great-grandmother, who would be out then, leaving the village without the right people to cut down a monster.

"I'm coming," she shouted, trying to sound brave— trying to feel brave. She was running as fast as she could, but it was hard to breathe, and her legs were slowing down. She gasped and pushed on.

Turning into the village, she saw chaos. Between the bright white curves of their homes, people were running every which way. She saw her mother, standing near the garden. She was leaning down, gesturing with her hands while she spoke with Peter Pan. Sashi was flying circles above their heads. Then her mother saw Tiger Lily and started waving her over, but Tiger Lily couldn't move.

In a flash, Peter took off on foot: "Come on, you big bully. I'm right here!" He raced to the clearing among the homes, running in circles, leaving the ground and spinning up and up, then touching down again and again gracefully. When she could move again, Tiger Lily pushed through the running people and walked toward her friend.

"Tiger Lily," he called out when he saw her. "Stay back!"

And then she saw it: chasing him was the biggest brown bear she had ever laid eyes on. Just then, it laid eyes on her.

"Oh," she sighed. "It's a bear, not a monster." But then the bear took two massive gallops in her direction and stood on its hind legs. It was so big it blocked out the sky. Tiger Lily felt tiny. She hoped her family wouldn't see what would happen to her next. She hoped it would be over fast. She could feel the bear's breath, like hot, rancid wind, as it growled down at her, its massive paws raised, claws out like so many knives. She closed her eyes.

"Hey, you hairy coward, over here!" Sashi flew circles around the creature's head so quickly, scattering so much glittery dust, it got dizzy trying to follow her movement. And Tiger Lily peeked just in time to see Peter Pan land on the thing's shoulder and poke it in the eye.

Then both Sashi and Peter were off, and the bear followed them, growling in frustration.

"Lily, get the raft," Peter shouted.

"What?"

"The raft! Bring the raft to the beach. Hurry!"

"What are you going to do with a raft?" She knew the bear was causing trouble, but something must have set it off. Still, what good was a raft?

She was confused, but the bear had run off so fast and hard the ground shook. Just then, the Lost Boys finally caught up, falling over each other to come to a stop.

"Where'd it go?" one twin asked.

"Yeah, where?" the other added.

"I . . . I don't know." Tiger Lily was not used to being scared. She had never frozen up like that, had never felt so small, so helpless—and just when her village needed her. Peter needed her, too. That bear was still after him.

"We have to get the raft," she instructed the Boys, snapping out of her reverie. "Quick. It's over in the woods by the hunt shack."

"Oh, boy, more running," Nibs panted. His glasses

slid down his sweaty nose. Determined to keep going, he flipped on his fox hood, attached to the old onesie pajamas he wore like a cloak, and took off after Tiger Lily.

They hadn't used the old raft for months, and it took them a bit to find where exactly they'd hidden it.

"Here! It's here!" Curly was waving her arms wildly from a patch of bramble bushes.

"Get it to the beach," Tiger Lily yelled as they all descended on the craft and wrenched it free from the weeds and branches grown over its rough construction. Together they pulled it out of the bushes and carried its awkward weight down to the sandy shore.

"What now?" Curly huffed, sitting on its corner, her shoes in the wet sand.

"Now we wait," Tiger Lily answered. She paced, listening in all directions, watching the tree line. No Sashi, no Peter . . . and no bear appeared. It had been too long. . . . Finally . . .

"There," she said, pointing to the east, where the branches snapped and waved like mad as Peter, followed closely by the giant bear, crashed out onto the beach.

"In the water . . . put it in the water!" Peter shouted, but somehow, in classic Pan style, he was still smiling, like this was all one big game.

Tiger Lily and the Lost Boys struggled to push the flat wooden raft—really just large branches lashed together with rope—into the waves. But finally, as it began to float, it became lighter.

"Hold it! Hooold it," Peter instructed, running zigzags to keep the creature on his tail. When he was no more than ten feet away, he shouted, "Now, run!"

The children scattered in all directions. For a moment, it looked like the bear would go after little Nibs, whose fox ears bobbed as he ran. But Tiger Lily saw just in time and, without pausing, whistled, high and loud, catching the animal's attention. She jumped up and down. "Over here!" Better it was after her than Nibs.

That gave Peter the chance to leap and bop the bear right on the snout. "Take that!"

It roared and swiped out with one of those enormous paws, just missing the boy—in fact, tearing a series of thin slits in the front of his shirt. Instead of scaring Peter, this made him laugh. "Good one, fuzzy."

With the bear back in pursuit, Peter landed on the

raft and danced about on light feet. "Well, come get me, then. I have nowhere left to go."

The enraged bear, practically foaming at the mouth, wasn't thinking, wasn't paying attention to anything other than the boy. Sashi flew just over Peter, making a big show to keep the bear focused, dropping pixie dust as she did. The edge of the raft still rested on the shore, but as the bear clambered on board and moved to its green-clad target, the entire floating object pushed off the shore and onto the Neversea with a whoosh.

And just like that, Sashi and Peter, now dusted with pixie dust, flew high into the sky, staying just above the little craft so the bear wouldn't see how far and fast it was floating away from land. By the time it did, the raft unsteady on the bobbing waves, it was too late. The bear was trapped and sailing out farther and farther from the beach.

"Smell ya later. Be sure to stop in and see ole Captain Hook," Peter said with a wave. "Tell him I sent ya!"

"Wait!" Tiger Lily was frantic. "You can't do that! What's going to happen to it?"

Sashi flew over to Tiger Lily. "Don't worry. The raft was your mother's idea. She told us, back at the village.

The tide will carry it to the other shore, by the forest, safe and sound."

"My mother?" Tiger Lily was watching the animal sail away. Curiously, it sat down on its haunches, as if it were going for a leisurely ride.

"Yeah, she said the bear got all riled up after it got caught in an old fishing net by accident," Sashi continued. "She couldn't find you, so she told me and Peter what to do."

The Lost Boys clapped and cheered from the shore. Tiger Lily let out all the air in her lungs and, tired though she was, started back to check on her village. The bear was gone; the people were safe. That was good. But she hadn't been the one to save them. And that made her feel very bad indeed.

There was a big feast that evening. Of course Peter took the opportunity to tell the daring tale of his triumph for anyone who wanted to hear it. The Lost Boys were only too happy to reenact the whole scene for the village, with Nibs in his furry cloak playing the role of the monstrous bear. Tiger Lily kept her distance. She sat under her favorite tree, away from the fire. That was where Gee found her. He walked over, a tall boy with his long hair pulled into a single braid. He had a big smile on his friendly face.

"Hey there. Your parents were wondering where you went," he said as he sat down next to her. They had grown up in the same community, and he knew better than to imagine she would follow him back to the gathering that easily. Tiger Lily did things in her own time.

"I just don't feel like hearing about Peter's great save again," she said, sighing. She hated that it looked like she was jealous. In truth, it was more than that. She felt small next to his big story—too small to be important. She knew she should be with the others, celebrating her friend's bravery and quick thinking, but she couldn't do it without feeling bad.

"Hey, you were a part of that whole rescue," Gee said consolingly. "He's not leaving that out. I only heard it the first four times he told it, so I should know. . . ."

Lily laughed, and Gee pushed her with his shoulder. She nudged him back. "Yes, he sure can tell a story," she said.

"Never seems to run out of wind, that one."

They sat in silence for a bit. It was comfortable, that silence. It gave her a chance to come up with the words to explain what was really bothering her. "I should have done better. I wasn't brave."

There. She had said it out loud. It felt like sharing a secret, but one she was ashamed of.

"Oh, come on, now," Gee said. "I wasn't exactly front and center, either, you know."

"And where were you?" she asked him. She already knew the answer.

"I was rounding up the spooked horses," he replied.

"Exactly. Single-handedly corralling scared horses isn't exactly standing still hoping you don't collapse with fear."

She realized what she had said as soon as she'd said it, but it was too late to take it back. Eyes wide, she looked at Gee, wondering if he'd heard her.

"You? Collapse with fear? Never."

He laughed, not at her but with her. His laugh was big and full of joy. It made her laugh, and she was grateful to have such a good friend right then.

"Here you are!"

Her mother approached and stood in front of them, blocking out the light from the big fire, where the shadows of Lost Boys played out the final scenes of the battle. "We were looking for you. We sent Gee, but I see he decided to hide with you instead of bringing you back."

Her mother was beautiful—the most beautiful woman Tiger Lily had ever seen. She was tall and kind, and that kindness lived in every part of her body. People loved to be around her for that reason. But Tiger Lily wasn't ready to feel better—not yet. She still needed some time to sit with her remorse and her doubts.

"Take Gee and go eat, Mother. I'll be there in a minute."

"You will, my girl?" Her mother ran a soft hand over her daughter's face, as if wiping away her worry.

"Yes, I'm fine. I'll be right there."

"All right, then. You heard her." She motioned to the boy, who stood up reluctantly. "Sometimes a girl just needs space."

She put her arm around Gee, and together they walked off across the grass.

Tiger Lily sat there for a while, long enough for her mother and her friend to return to the fire, for the fire to die down, and for the people to start returning to their own homes. She was falling asleep in the quiet dark when she heard the Lost Boys, Sashi, and Peter going past, on their way to their own homes. They didn't see her there.

"I hope she's all right," Sashi jingled. "Her mother said she was having alone time."

"She's better than all right. She saved my skin today," Nibs interjected.

"Yes, she just seemed a little . . . down," Sashi finished.

"She just needs to get more get-up-and-fight is all," Peter said brightly, playfully sparring with the darkness around him. "She needs some of the ole one-two puncheroos!"

"She's plenty fighty," the twins said together.

"Yes," answered Peter. "Maybe it's just time for her to visit the old Andon for some advice."

He danced through the grass as though in a fight.

"What's an Andon?" Curly asked through a yawn.

"Beats me," Nibs answered, stifling his own yawn. "Hey, I caught your sleepiness. Cut out the yawning!"

Peter Pan stretched his arms above his head. They were all a little sleepy. "I'm off to London with Tink tomorrow, so let Tiger Lily know, wouldya, Sashi? So she checks on the Boys."

Tiger Lily stayed where she was, watching her friends make their way back into the woods, where they would go their separate ways—Sashi to her cozy home and the others to theirs. After hearing that Peter thought she could use more fight, she felt smaller than ever. Soon she dragged herself to her bed and fell into a dreamless sleep.

Chapter Two

The morning after the bear incident, Tiger Lily wanted to spend more time alone, so she went to the caves under Skull Rock. She needed to think about what had happened—figure out why she had frozen up like that, and just when she was needed. She loved to visit the caves. She had spent so many hours there that she could even navigate them in the dark. She knew exactly where to find a finger grip and where to place her feet.

Hidden from the untrained eye and winding through many parts of Neverland, the caves were an underground secret her community had kept through the years, a place to hide from the pirates in times past. They were still important, even though the people didn't need to use them anymore—not since the battles had stopped, the pirates had taken the *Jolly Roger* farther into the sea, and peace had returned to Neverland. Now the caves were used for remembering, and Tiger Lily thought that was just as important.

The walls were tall and curved and covered in huge murals that stretched up overhead. To Tiger Lily and to her thirteen-year-old eyes, this was the most important place in all the world. She studied the figures and scenes—some bigger than she was, some tiny and dim—with awe and pride.

"They really could paint," she whispered, marveling at the curved lines of horses and the bright faces of the people.

Her whisper echoed in the tunnels and came back to her ears like a song. Everything was repeated down here. It made everything sound more important. This was where her great-great-grandmother took her to teach her about her ancestors, about the island, about who she was and who she could be, about how they alone could choose to grow older. It was here that she learned about her responsibilities as an Indigenous woman—to take care of her extended family and the lands on which they lived.

Even though she was the only person in the cave, she never felt alone here. She heard her grandmother's voice in her head: *You come from greatness, so your responsibilities are a gift, a way of being connected to the greatness of those who came before you.*

That made her think about the first time she had missed the community fishing trip.

Once a year, a giant school of whitefish made their way through the waters right by Neverland. No one knew exactly where they came from, though there were stories.

"They come down through the stars, swimming the universe to get to us. They come from the place we were before we were here, and they know we are hungry for original foods," one of her aunties had explained.

"Who would travel that far just to get eaten?" she whispered to Gee, who had sat beside her that night while they heard the old stories. He stifled a laugh.

Wherever they came from and however they got here, the whitefish came in great numbers—so many you could hear them hum from the shore. The people rode on their horses, pulling wagons stacked with light fishing boats made of birch bark and sealed with sap down to the water's edge nearby wherever the fish were spotted that year. They made offerings to the fish and sang songs to honor their sacrifice so that the people might eat well for another year. Then they followed the swarm in whatever direction they led as they twisted and turned in the water, never going too fast or too deep for the fishers to catch them. The people would gather as many as they needed to sustain the community for another year, until they would go out to do it all over again. It took about four full turns of the sun and moon to complete.

A few seasons earlier, Tiger Lily had asked to be excused.

"I go every year. I don't want to go this year!"

"My girl, why not?" This was the way her grandmother dealt with her outbursts, always leading with concern before showing annoyance or disappointment. "Are you not feeling well?"

"I'm fine," Tiger Lily admitted. She had thought at first she would use illness as an excuse, but she didn't like lying to or worrying her grandmother. "I just don't want to. I'm not a fisher, and I don't want to become one."

"But don't you want to feed your people? That's an important job, one of the most important."

Tiger Lily had trouble explaining it. She was frustrated, moody. Even sitting there trying to explain it with words she didn't have made her all itchy under her skin. "I feel like I'm supposed to be doing something else."

"Ah, I see." Grandma sat down on her favorite stump seat and smiled. "You're figuring it out."

Tiger Lily sat down beside her, leaning into her soft side. She loved the way her grandmother's skin felt, the way she smelled, like good work and happy memories. "Figuring what out?"

"You're figuring *you* out. It happens one day. You wake up and all of a sudden there is so much to figure out." She laughed. It was a gentle laughter that didn't diminish or mock. "I understand. How about you take this year off? Figuring out you is important work. It's the work of growing up."

That answer had not brought comfort to Tiger Lily. There was that phrase again: *growing up*. Those words meant she had to make a decision: leave childhood and maybe even her childhood friends and jump ahead a few years, or stay exactly the same. Neither one felt right. She didn't want things to change, but then again, what was the point of staying the same?

"Why would anyone want to get older? I know why we have to stop being babies, and I'm glad I made the decision to become an older child, but growing any older than this?" She touched her own shoulders to indicate herself. "Why would anyone do that?"

Her grandmother allowed the moment of frustration. She didn't tell her to stop fidgeting in the dirt or to accept things for what they were. She just held space for Tiger Lily to feel the way she felt. Then she responded.

"Neverland is a place of imagination, right? So what if having your whole family tree spread out from your roots, reaching into the sky while still being firmly held in the ground, is the most wonderful thing you can imagine?" She sounded happy. Tiger Lily turned to look up into her face and saw that there were tears in her eyes. "Growing up means growing out and growing in, and being all things at once—at least for us. We are so lucky."

Tiger Lily leaned harder into the woman, who wrapped an arm over her shoulders. "I am the luckiest woman who ever lived."

Tiger Lily had gotten out of fishing that year and every year since. And every year since, she had wondered who exactly she was meant to be, for her village and for herself, and if that also meant having to grow into an adult.

Now a different voice came to her in the jingling of fairy chatter, a sound like tiny bells: "Lily, you down there?"

The question echoed off the walls so it became a mini chorus on its own. She recognized the voice as belonging to Sashi. Of course Sashi had found her; she knew her better than anyone else. They had been friends for ages, ever since Lily had found a giant mushroom with a little door cut into the side and knocked on it. It was Sashi who answered, and though it took some time for Lily to learn her distinct fairy language, they were friends almost immediately. Sashi taught her the language, but also about art and how to wear it. The fairy took her fashion very seriously, changing her hair and her outfits as often as she could.

One rainy season, a small flood washed out the

part of the woods where Sashi lived on her own, and sent her mushroom spinning along the fast-rushing water. Tiger Lily helped collect her things, and the two spent days searching for a new home for Sashi. They decided up high was safer than on the ground, and once they found the perfect spot, the two friends made it a proper home together. Though many of the fairies lived in Pixie Hollow, some fairies liked to live alone, since they needed lots of space to fly and sing, though they also came together often to celebrate as a community.

Since then, they'd traversed the entire island a thousand times, searching out adventure, looking for new fun to have, and trying to take care of the creatures who needed them.

"Coming!" Tiger Lily answered Sashi's call now. She stood up and brushed the dirt off her fringed pants. She slowly spun around in place to again take in the cave paintings, everything that had been left and taken care of so that one day a girl, just like her, could be surrounded by her very own history.

She nodded to the portrait of a young woman with a long braid swirling around her like a storm. The woman sat atop a white steed, just like Tiger Lily's own Pony. She was tall from her mount, imposing and serious but with something mischievous about her face. There were other pictures of this woman down here: in one she was lassoing the moon; in another she was chasing a herd of snakes from the village.

"See you soon," Tiger Lily told the image.

She knew this woman was her very own grandmother; the older woman had told her as much, and besides, she could feel it in her bones. Belonging was a thing that lived in your marrow, that whispered to you with every cell in your body. It had to be the best feeling in the whole world. It was a kind of love that never stopped holding you.

She clambered up an incline toward the sunlight and emerged through a brush-covered opening into the bright day. The world up here was a riot of green and blue, shades of the plants that wound their way around the forest, and of the sky that bloomed big and bright above them. The air smelled like a hundred different flowers and, from far away, good smoke. Someone was preparing food. It must be nearing the midday meal. Time was measured by activity here—mealtime, chore time, sleep time. They were the only things that divided up the days before the moon called them all to lie down and dream.

"How are you today?" Sashi was lounging on a berry tree, with red juice lining her mouth. Obviously, she had already eaten her way through a bunch. She passed her forearm over her face, only smearing the juice onto her cheek. "You know . . . after the bear . . ."

"I'm fine," Tiger Lily said. She really was. The murals always helped put things into perspective. Being surrounded by images of who she was, who her people were, always made her feel the kind of pride that brought bravery. She knew she could be brave enough to make tough decisions and to learn from her mistakes. Now that she was clear of the cave, she stretched back to her full height and laughed at her little friend.

Sashi sat up. "Good, because I'm bored."

"It's not even lunchtime and already you're bored?"

Sashi shrugged her tiny shoulders, the movement setting the bells on her purple dress tinkling. She'd sewn those bells on herself, having fallen in love with the way they clanged loudly when she was fierce, or whispered soft metal songs when she was full of grace. Sashi loved making clothes to match her moods. She'd recently started crafting jewelry out of the bits and bobs she found around the island.

"What can I say? I have a lot of energy. I've already cleaned my place, made a new bracelet, flown to the Lost Boys' camp to make sure they're staying out of trouble, and then found you."

"Are they?" Tiger Lily asked, stretching her arms above her head, working out the kinks from crouching.

"Are they what?"

"Staying out of trouble—especially after yesterday?" She knew it was a long shot; Peter and the Lost Boys were known for trouble. They were either getting into trouble or telling stories about the trouble they'd been in. They told these stories like they were great adventurers and not just a bunch of bumbling kids with too much time on their hands.

"Well, Peter's off to London, and the Boys are still sleeping, so all good for today, so far. But their place . . ." Sashi pinched her nose with her fingers. "Yuck!"

Tiger Lily often wondered if the Lost Boys would even manage without the inhabitants of Neverland—like herself—who made it their job to check up on them. Delivering meals and stitching pants were things the more responsible citizens did for the Boys, jobs that were passed along and shared among them.

Though over the years, the Boys had come to know not to cross Tiger Lily—not because they feared her, but because they looked up to her. They listened to her orders and carried out her tasks, for the most part. They wanted to be like her—responsible, respected, even clean. If she'd let them, they'd be with her all the time.

Because they looked up to her so much, Tiger Lily felt especially bad that she nearly hadn't been able to protect them the previous day. She tried not to think about it. Her grandmother always said dwelling on what made you feel bad only made you feel worse.

"Well, as long as they bathe before they try to come see us again . . ." she said to Sashi, who laughed, too.

The two friends wound their way through the forest and down to the beach. The brush was thick, and flowered vines reached out to connect the trees to one another, making one big braid out of the green. To an outsider, it would seem impossible to get through. But Tiger Lily and Sashi knew every nook in it.

One would think that after traveling the same paths so many times, they would stop noticing the way the sun got caught in every raindrop on each leave so that the entire woods shone like jewels. That perhaps they wouldn't see that some paths changed their destination, one day ending at the swamp, and the next day ending at Mermaid Lagoon. But every day they marveled at the place they called home. And every day they were rewarded with new joys.

Sashi stopped here and there to smell a flower or take a bite out of a soft fruit hanging off the trees. She hummed almost constantly, little songs she heard from the birds or remembered from the bugs who sang her to sleep each night. Sashi was always in motion, always making sound. She snored when she slept, and even that was a gravelly kind of music.

"So what were you doing down there, anyway?" asked Sashi.

Tiger Lily stalled. "In the caves?"

"Yes, you only go down there when you have to really think about something. So then, what were you thinking about?"

Tiger Lily paused. She wasn't sure she wanted to talk about it yet. Talking about things, giving them words and names, made them more real. And so far, she had needed this thing to stay not real. She hoped her friend would understand.

She shrugged. "Just things. I'll tell you about it when I'm ready."

Sashi wasn't used to not knowing everything about her friend, but she shrugged. She understood that people needed to work on their own time. "As long as you're all right . . ."

"I am."

"Okay, then . . . race you to the water!"

Tiger Lily smiled, grateful. She would have hugged Sashi right then and there if the fairy hadn't been itching for a race. Plus, it was a curious thing, trying to hug a fairy. They were so much smaller and so full of light and movement it felt like trying to embrace a bird midflight.

They could hear the waves from where they were, which meant the beach was just ahead. Both took off—Sashi flying, Tiger Lily running—and they arrived at the same time on the white sand.

Sashi flew over the shore, twisting in a bright somersault in midair. "I love it here!"

Tiger Lily bent over, her hands on her knees, to catch her breath after their sudden sprint. She looked at her friend and then over the beach and smiled. The water was deep blue but filled with light patches of turquoise, so she knew it wasn't very deep in those spots. On the horizon were the peaks and crags of mountains. From this angle, she could see the place her caves led to—the dreaded Skull Rock, named after its shape, like a human skull with wide eyeholes and a dome. These far-off formations looked like shadows against the clear sky.

The weather was very rarely anything but splendid all year round. Even the breezes here were warm and fragrant. The rainy season brought new vegetation and warm days. A line of small orange crabs scuttled over the wet sand, their eyes large and wary. The sound of their claws snapping open and shut was like music, a kind of marching band keeping step and applauding themselves with small sharp snips.

"It's the most beautiful place there is," Tiger Lily agreed. Sometimes she wanted to cry just looking around her, good tears, grateful tears. The biggest feelings broke through with those tears. Her uncle told her happy tears were how the Neversea had come into being: a collection of joyous tears had all pooled into one giant ocean.

She shimmied out of her clothes, down to the swimming suit she wore underneath. For Sashi and

Tiger Lily, swimming was an important part of the day. They went almost every day, even when it rained, so she was always prepared. She gathered up her long hair, twisted it, and tied it in a big loose knot at the nape of her neck. Sashi, the more prepared of the two, tied her curls back with a strip of ribbon, the same purple as her dress, that she kept tied to her wrist for just that purpose.

Sashi folded her dress neatly and laid it on a rock. Then she carefully collapsed her wings so they were flat against her back, her tongue sticking out of the corner of her mouth as she concentrated on pulling them in. It was like flexing a muscle, and it took some practice to do it right so that they weren't all creased later. She caught Tiger Lily gazing toward Skull Rock.

"What do you think the pirates are up to today?" Sashi asked.

Tiger Lily tensed and, holding her hand above her eyebrows, shifted to look over the blue expanse on either side of the mountains. She felt relief course through her when she found the horizon all clear— not a vessel or a sound out on the water, nothing to make her nervous, nothing to stop their leisurely swim.

"Who knows? As long as they're not around to bother us, I don't care."

The truth was she did care; she always cared. She felt like it was one of her responsibilities here, to her village and this land, to keep an eye on the scoundrels who organized under the loathsome Captain Hook. The pirates usually stayed far away from her community, but as her father reminded her, they never knew how or when things would change. If she wanted to get better at protecting her family and friends, maybe she should start by checking in on the pirates . . . just in case. She made a mental note to get Pony and ride the perimeter of the shoreline after lunch, just to see if they were around. She didn't trust the empty horizon, the full stillness.

"I get nervous when we can't even spot the ship," Sashi said, as if she could hear her friend's thoughts. "Who knows what they're up to when they aren't out here being loud and ridiculous?"

"Exactly," Tiger Lily agreed before she took off running down the sand. "That's why the Lost Boys aren't really dangerous to anyone but themselves—too loud."

She splashed into the water and dove underneath.

She opened her eyes underwater, gazing at the sun, now a mess of bright ribbons twisting above her. And for the first time that day, she completely relaxed, letting her arms loose so that they caught each push and pull of the waves.

In the water, she once more dwelled on what had sent her to the caves that morning: the nagging feeling of uncertainty. Tiger Lily was truly considering leaving her childhood behind and growing older than she was now. As her grandmother had taught her, it was a process that belonged to her community alone on Neverland, the place where no one grew up, where time held still, where you could live in imagination and joy forever, never aging a day. Only they, the people of her village, could wish themselves into different ages, becoming adults—parents, grandparents, even great-great-grandparents if they chose.

She rememberd her grandmother's exact words, years ago: "It's a gift. We have always had the choice to grow up, because for us, being an ancestor is the greatest honor one could receive, the best thing we could hope for. But it is still a choice—one you'll have to make for yourself."

She knew from her grandmother, and from the cave paintings that told their collective story, that many years earlier her community had wished for this ability, had dreamed of it. And Neverland was first and foremost a place of dreams, a land made up of childhood wishes. So the island had listened to their request.

And here she was, facing one decision in a longer line of decisions that might one day make her just like her grandmother. Did she really want to grow up more? Sure, she had grown from a baby when she wanted to walk and talk and be her own person, and then from a small child into the bigger girl she was now. But this was different. This was the "big change." It meant leaving childhood and entering young adulthood.

She loved being this age—the freedom, the messiness, the chance to be carefree and cared for. But she also knew that young adulthood offered its own gifts: being more aware, longing for new things, plus maybe being a better protector, like the kind that could single-handedly take on a bear.

She worried more than anything about whether growing up would mean that she would be leaving her friends behind. That she couldn't bear. She had never really been alone in her life, and the thought of it was too much. At least if she stayed the same, she would always have her friends.

Pulling herself through the water with long strokes, observing the schools of colorful fish that watched her pass, Tiger Lily was able to let all that go and just be. Right then, life was full of adventure. And she wasn't sure she'd ever be ready for that to change.

Chapter Three

Tiger Lily got back to her village several hours later. But she didn't arrive empty-handed. She and Sashi had gathered apples along the way, enough to fill the burlap sack she kept tied to Pony's saddle in case she came across anything to carry home. Well, Sashi had pointed them out, and Tiger Lily had picked them. Sashi wasn't able to lift the weight of an apple. Lily hoped this would keep her grandmother from giving her a talking-to about staying out all day without checking in.

She had just entered village territory when someone stepped onto the path behind her, slipping out from the trees. She smiled and slowed down, hearing the approach before any words were spoken.

"Did you check the traps while you were out?" Gee had snuck up behind her, trying to make her jump—but he should have known better. Tiger Lily was a hunter, and as such, she had trained her ears to hear the slightest movements. And her tracking skills, which included moving without sound, were better than Gee's. Some people thought it was just sounds creatures made that alerted hunters. But Tiger Lily knew it was also the absence of sound. Things grew quiet when shadows passed over them.

"I did. Nothing yet." She answered smoothly, letting him know he had failed to startle her. "Guess you'll have to go out and check yourself before dinner, kid."

He sighed loudly, kicking at the ground. "Fine."

She didn't like seeing her friend disappointed, not even about something small and silly like this. Tiger Lily smiled, reached into her bag, and tossed him a crisp apple. He caught it in the air and smiled back, rubbing the fruit against the front of his shirt.

"When you go, maybe I could go with you?" she suggested.

"Oh, I'm sorry, Gee, but Tiger Lily has work to do

here." Her grandmother walked into the clearing. Now, here was a person who could sneak up on anybody, especially her kin who were late for their chores.

Tiger Lily and Gee stood a little straighter. They weren't afraid of the older woman, but they were always eager to be their best around her. She was a true leader, and true leaders inspired their people to be the best versions of themselves without fear.

"Not cleaning, I hope," Lily responded before hugging her grandmother.

"No, my girl, not today. Though I haven't checked your place lately. You're not turning into one of Pan's Boys, are you? You've been spending quite a bit of time with them."

"No! But to be fair, they are getting better."

Grandma chuckled. "That's good news." She grew thoughtful. "Every child deserves to be watched over. Every child deserves to feel cared for."

Tiger Lily nodded. She agreed and didn't mind looking out for them, really—even if getting them to clean up after themselves was like trying to coax minnows into a straight line. They were always running off or even hiding if they thought they had a chance at escaping from the work.

"Not everyone is as lucky as you," Grandma said. "The Lost Boys are lost for several reasons. They have lost their parents and they have lost their sense of direction. Without direction, you tend to spin out in all ways at once."

Tiger Lily took this in. Her grandmother was good at reminding her about her responsibilities in a way that made them seem like an honor. "It's fine, Grandma. All good, no need to check my place . . ."

Tiger Lily threw her arm around the woman's shoulders and covered her words with her own to avoid getting into the state of her space. She had only just convinced her family that she needed her own tent; she wasn't about to lose the privilege over a messy bed. While orderly by nature, Tiger Lily was not finicky about things like folding or stacking, certainly not when there was so much to do outside her teepee.

Grandma laughed. She saw right through her, always did.

"Always so much to do, you," she said. "Always so busy. Tell me about your day, then."

Tiger Lily jumped into the tale. She loved spending time with her grandmother, and sometimes she chose her activities for the day based on what would make the better story to tell her later.

"I visited the caves to go see the family gallery. Then Sashi came and found me, and we went swimming. After that, we worked on our tree house—the one we're building out by the eastern woods near Crocodile Creek? I want to make it so that there are walls to paint on, like the caves, a place where people can come to see art and history and beautiful, brave things. And then we picked apples." She held up the sack. "I have enough to make sweets for the whole family."

"Good, good." Grandma got serious for a minute. "Any of Hook's men around today?"

"No, none that I could see." She wanted to tell her that she was going for a ride later with Pony, to patrol the beaches a bit just in case. She wanted to tell her, really, but she knew her grandmother would tell her not to go. So instead, she decided to keep that part to herself. She couldn't defy her grandmother once she'd told her not to do something. Better not to give her the chance to say no. "I hope we never see them again."

"Agreed. But I don't like when they hide away. Mind you, I don't want to see them, either," Grandma said, shuddering. "You just be careful. Don't be out there too much. It's better when the likes of them don't take notice of the likes of you."

There was something even more serious in her voice now. Her words had a darker edge to them. Tiger Lily understood that her grandmother was reminding her that for her, a young girl from their community, the world was not always safe—another good reason to grow up. She was silent for a few seconds, then broke the somber mood.

"Maybe I should just join them," she joked. "You know, just become one of them so I can keep a close eye on everything. And who knows? Maybe it's fun. Maybe I was born for a life of rot on the high seas."

Tiger Lily moved away, dropping the sack at her feet. She arched her back, closed one eye, and hitched her shoulders up to her ears. She turned suddenly to her grandmother, snarling.

"Argh, matey, I'm Cap'n Hook, see, and I have come for your gold!" She staggered toward the older woman, screwing up her face in a comical grimace. "You, little girl, give me all yer goods or I'll cut 'em outta ya with this!"

They both laughed.

"Oh, you are too good at that," the older woman said.

"Imitating pirates is my special talent," Tiger Lily responded, taking a deep and sarcastic bow from the waist.

"I don't know about that. Today, I think, preparing the seeds is going to become your special talent," her grandmother said. Then she became serious for another moment. "You need to keep up with your learning."

The girl sighed. "Seeds, though? That's so boring. Can't I go out on the hunt?"

"Of course you can, but not today, not when that bear might have made it back to shore. I'd rather you weren't out in the bush. Today we are preparing seeds, and you are joining us." She reached for her granddaughter's hand. "Not everything can be fast and exciting. Sometimes it's slow and mindful. But both are important when they feed the community."

Her grandmother knew this was the way to get her to participate. Everyone knew that Tiger Lily loved her community, that she would do anything for the small group of brilliant individuals who lived here on their beloved land.

The village was set up in a circle with birch-bark

structures, many with their own individual firepits for cooking or tanning or praying. Some families lived in smaller semicircles, their homes sitting close together. These groups shared a larger firepit among them, using their space better and offering the opportunity to gather each day. Being around family was the best place to be, so most of the village was laid out like this.

Because life in Neverland had been peaceful for many years, the community had truly settled in, though they still favored the teepee homes that would typically have been used when moving was a way of life. The village was also full of garden plots with mature plants and vines heavy with fruits and vegetables. There were areas between trees covered with smoky tanned hides to keep out the sun or the rain so that the people could work together shucking corn or braiding sweet-grass. There were voices and color and laughter. Some artists had carved magnificent sculptures—deer and florals and even ancestors, like in the cave drawings. These adorned the outside of the Council Hall, the place where they gathered to celebrate and occasionally to mourn. The Council Hall was the central meeting place, where all were welcome, from the youngest to the oldest among them.

Around the circle were the outbuildings, where the hunters kept their traps and where the hides were harvested. There was also a large lean-to with rain barrels and soft hay bedding they had built at one end of a lush field full of sweet-tasting flowers and shady trees. This was where their beloved horses, including Tiger Lily's own Pony, grazed when they weren't out riding around Neverland.

The whole community was a beautiful place nestled in the woods right near the water, and Tiger Lily felt lucky every time she walked its tall gardens and winding paths. And that day she was walking the space with her favorite person, her brave and beloved grandmother.

"You should know by now how to secure the seeds and keep them safe until planting time. And also which seed goes into the ground at what time." Her grandmother spoke to her between greeting those they passed along the path. She was a respected Elder, so everyone made sure to stop and acknowledge her no matter what they were doing. Sometimes, it made going for a stroll with her an all-day event.

Tiger Lily was quiet for a moment. Then she said, "I've been thinking lately, about the decision I have to make. Would that mean many more responsibilities?"

"Well, my girl, if you do decide to age, then yes, there will be more responsibilities. More freedom and new joy, but weighing you to this ground will be those responsibilities. So you don't just . . . float away." She made her hands into butterfly wings and moved them toward the sky.

Lily watched that movement until the sun made her close her eyes. It didn't seem that bad, just floating like that—free, without weight, just the warm sky and all Neverland below.

"It's just that things change. This one is different from all others—before or after. It's leaving behind my childhood." Tiger Lily was sad just saying it. "And I can never get it back. But I also know that it would mean I could be stronger, be a better protector. I'm just not sure it will be worth the cost."

"That is true. Once it's passed, it is just that—the past. But there are things to look forward to. Growing up isn't all about strength and sacrifice."

"Like what?"

"Like being a grown-up. Being a parent, a grand-parent." Grandma touched her own chest just above her heart. "It's been the greatest time of my life."

"No offense, but that was so long ago." Tiger Lily

continued quickly, "I don't mean that as a bad thing. It's just . . . when was the last time someone did it? I've never seen anyone here age out of childhood—not since I can remember. I think it must be sad."

"Sad? Why sad?"

"Because it's the one time you lose something."

Her grandmother took her hand. "What is it you think you're going to lose that's so precious, my girl?"

Tiger Lily wasn't sure what the right words were. It was more a bunch of feelings—big, bright, beautiful feelings that were sometimes scary but mostly amazing. She used the only word that might even begin to fit. "Magic. You lose your magic."

Walking now, she saw all the color being sucked out of her days. Certainty would chase away adventure. Responsibility would chase away dreams. Yes, she would be able to protect the village, like Peter had, but . . .

Her grandmother steered her to a covered spot laid with woven mats and crowded with others of all genders, each learning from someone beside them who already knew. They took from the central pile of blooms past their prime and carefully removed shiny trapped seeds, peeling back drying husks and pods to free them.

Two women helped her grandmother sit on a short

stack of mats before settling back into their own spots. Tiger Lily sat on her grandmother's right. The group quieted, still working, and waited for the woman to speak.

"A seed is a promise," she said. "A promise that there will be a tomorrow from the work of today. So it is happy work, to be the hand between those two times—between today and tomorrow."

Tiger Lily picked a red bloom from the pile, the leaves withered and the stalk mushy. *Is this what it is to get old?* she thought, twisting the flower in her fingers. *Turning into this?*

"Isn't it sad, though?" she asked out loud.

"Sad?" Grandma regarded her with soft eyes. "How is it sad, my girl?"

Lily raised the flower to her nose. There was only an earthy scent of decay, no more perfume. "It's dead."

Grandma smiled, taking the bloom from her granddaughter. She held it between her fingers and cracked the plant in two, then picked out tiny round seeds. "It isn't dead. Here . . ." She showed Lily the small specks, light as air, that clung to her fingerprints. "See? There is no death. Just cycles. This is its next cycle. Everything has its time, and around and around it goes."

Tiger Lily picked one seed from the group and held it close to her eye. Tiny. Perfect. So fragile.

"So the older flower kind of protects the little ones?"

Grandma smiled big. "They always do."

Chapter Four

This was her favorite feeling in the entire world: riding her white steed, Pony, before the sun disappeared over the horizon. She'd helped prepare dinner and served the Elders their meals before anyone else lined up for food; then she'd snuck away. Well, she didn't exactly sneak away. Her mother and grandmother knew she was going out riding, even if she did leave out the detail that she was going to scout. She knew it was important to make sure someone knew where you were going in case you needed help, so she told them her route.

Gee had spotted her as she'd slipped away, and he'd stuck out his tongue at her. He had been cleaning out the old traps and stacking them alongside the hunter's shed. She'd waved back, knowing he was sore about not joining her, and then set Pony into a gallop. A part of her had wanted to ask him to come with her.

But at the moment, Tiger Lily wanted to be alone again. Just her and Pony. She wanted time to think.

There was no breeze that could match the wind Tiger Lily made herself on top of a fast horse at the end of a day. It blew away every stressful thought, left worries squirming in the dust behind. They sped through a field dotted with fat yellow blooms and then slowed to pick their way through the woods—until they burst back out into the open across a grassy expanse, both glad to pick up speed again. Soon Tiger Lily could smell the sea, and her breathing slowed to take it in. It was like the air got thicker and clearer at the same time. This was the best kind of floating, with a strong horse under her and the water ahead. She closed her eyes.

Pony grunted and tossed his head a bit, the movement as small as a shiver but enough that his attentive rider felt it. She opened her eyes and looked ahead. And there, near the beach, were two figures in a boat.

She pulled on the reins, not hard. Pony knew what she wanted with the smallest of movements, and he slowed, turning in a wide circle to stop himself. She clicked her tongue and lowered her body against his back so that, from far away, if anyone saw them, Pony would look like a riderless horse—just one of the wild ones that galloped around the island. In this position, they made for the trees.

Once they were behind a cluster of willows, Tiger Lily dismounted.

"Stay," she whispered to Pony, who lowered his head in understanding. Really, she didn't have to say the word out loud; he could read her motions, understand her moods. One morning when she was sick in bed, he'd left the field and ended up inside her tent, swishing his tail with worry so that a pile of newly washed clothes was blown out into the yard. Oh, her grandmother had a fit over that!

Still crouched, she made her way closer to the beach and settled in the tall grass just past the sand, hidden in the shadow of a small mound. A bee buzzed angrily by her ear, letting her know she had disturbed its rest.

"Sorry," she whispered, softly waving it away without touching it. It was always best to have manners with Neverland bees. Luckily, this one accepted her apology and went on its way.

She looked out through the weeds. Now she could see the figures better. They were two men. When they began to talk, she could hear them, too, their voices loud and animated. That meant they were careless. Either they weren't up to anything and had nothing to hide, or they did have something to hide and were very, very dumb.

They were pirates; that much was clear already from their clothes and their smell. For people who spent their lives on the water, pirates sure didn't like to bathe. The shorter one, who guided a small wooden boat to the shore, looked young and had long red hair, tied back with a piece of leather. His blouse was yellowed brown, and his short pants were ragged at the cuffs, with one of the pockets stuffed with a slab of hard bread and the other hanging loose from its threads. Most important to note, a cutlass hung from his belt loop.

The taller one was huge, like the bear that had wandered into the village. His melon head was covered in straw-blond hair, cut blunt and awkward, probably with a dull blade. (Pirates were not known for their barber skills.) In place of a shirt, he wore only a peculiar jacket, formal almost, stiff, with stripes in the fabric and padding in the shoulders. Several gold chains hung around his neck, and a wide leather belt held up his ragged pants around his thick waist. He stood on the wet sand in soaked decrepit black boots.

"Hurry up, we gotta get this done before they see the boat's gone," the big one yelled.

"Or in case they notice us gone," the smaller one huffed, beaching the heavy boat.

"No one's gonna notice us gone. When do they ever notice us?" The tall one stretched, his thick arms resting on his lower back. "They wouldn't notice if we was on fire."

"Come on, now, it's not as bad as all that." The short man gave the boat a final push onto the solid ground and sat down on the edge, breathing heavily. "They'd put us out if we was on fire."

His friend laughed without humor. "Huh, yeah, maybe by tossing us overboard."

They paused for a moment, looking up and down the beach and catching their breath. Holding her own breath, Tiger Lily lowered her head behind the mound. How was it that pirates were always in such bad shape? Didn't they get any exercise rowing around all day?

"So how are we supposed to find it?" asked the smaller man.

"It's not gonna be easy," his companion replied. "You can't just happen upon the biggest treasure in Neverland without working for it."

Not again, she thought. Every few years, someone went looking for some fabled pot of gold or casket of jewels, and usually that someone was one of the pirates. It was part of the mythology of this place, that there were untold riches just waiting for some person to dig them up. The pirates existed for treasure, it seemed. Maybe that was why they stayed in Neverland; why they came in the first place. Well, that and the fact that they could live however they wanted—dirtier than the Lost Boys, louder than the birds—on Skull Rock.

Tiger Lily looked out again. Now the pirates hurried down the beach away from where she crouched. Before they got out of range, she overheard the short one ask, "You really think we can find the Andon on our own?"

"The Andon?" Tiger Lily whispered to herself. "Why is that so familiar?" She remembered Peter mentioning it the previous night, saying how she needed it, to get some more fight. Even as a memory, it still stung. She didn't like being examined and found lacking.

"If anyone can find it, Jolly, my boy, it's us," said the big one. "And we will leave this place with the one thing everyone in every land wants and will pay any amount for: eternal youth!"

He threw his arms wide open in excitement, accidentally slapping his friend's cheek as he did.

She wanted to follow them, but the landscape was too flat here. Surely even these two would notice her if she tailed them along the open beach. She watched them from her nook until they hit the shrubs, and she knew they could only be going one place: into the swamp.

She made her way back to Pony and swung up into the saddle. "Okay, Pony, let's see what we can see."

She clicked her tongue, and off they went, galloping over the grass, avoiding the sand where a horse's prints might be spotted, then looping around the perimeter of the great swamp to find a safer way in, one where they could avoid both the pirates and the dangers that lurked in the deeper parts of the mire.

"Those fools are going to be real torn up going into the swamp from the beach. That is, if they manage to avoid the crocodiles," she mused. A part of her wanted to shout out to them, to stop them. But another knew that wouldn't stop them. It would only put her more at risk.

She left Pony safe and sound, chewing grass seed on solid ground, and made for the darker shrubs that led into the swamp. Before she pushed into the greenery, she looked up at the sky, where the light blue was sliding into deeper navy and a streak of pink reached out from the west.

"I won't be long," she whispered to her horse. "Gotta head back before the stars come out, or Grandma will have both our hides."

Pony looked up and whinnied. Even he knew better than to mess with an Elder.

Then Tiger Lily took a deep breath and walked into the dark.

Chapter Five

O f the many things Tiger Lily didn't understand about pirates, how they could be so clumsy was high on her list. Maybe it was just that on land they were completely out of their element. They were like hippopotamuses in boots—loud and destructive. Whatever the case, she had no trouble tracking the two men from the beach.

Branches snapped so loud that even the crickets stopped chirping, and they usually played their symphony through storms. The water splashed so high the frogs found logs to perch on out of reach, and they didn't move for predators. Every now and then, one man or the other would exclaim from the dense gloom:

"Rats in the bilge! My boot is stuck!"

"I can't get through here. It's mucky as Smee's best tea!"

"Argh! I heard something. Did you hear that? Is it a crocodile?"

She followed the sound of their misery, careful to step on solid ground and avoid the snakes that watched in silence from their holes and branches.

"You stay right where you are," she hissed to them as their beady eyes followed her every move. "And I'll try to stay out of your way, since I'm in your territory."

They watched her but made no slither, only popped their long forked tongues in her direction.

"Are you sure it's in here, Jukes?" asked the short one, Jolly.

"Jukes and Jolly," she murmured to herself. She thought she recognized Jukes. The village kept a running list of the pirates somewhere in the Council Hall, with Hook firmly pinned to the top. But Jukes was no slouch, either. Bill was his first name. He was a particularly nasty pirate, known for his massive size and brutish temper.

"Jukesy," Jolly called out again when he got no answer. "You know it's here, yeah?"

"Relax!" Bill Jukes replied. "I know it's here. I mean, I think so. They said it was in a place no one wants to go. And this surely is the one place no one wants to go, not even animals."

"You mean other than the crocs," Jolly whimpered.

Jukes sighed a sigh that ended in a kind of growl. "Oh, would you quit it with the crocs?"

There was a loud splash, as if something had been thrown, followed by a pained groan.

"Owww, why'd you do that?"

Now Tiger Lily could see them clearly: the short man rubbing the side of his head, the large one up to his knees in the murky water.

"Just keep your eyeballs peeled for anything that looks . . . out of place."

Jukes turned quickly, and Tiger Lily ducked behind a dead tree.

"What? Did you see something?" Jolly whispered.

"Not sure. Just . . . felt like we were being watched."

Tiger Lily held her breath. Her quick movement had splashed mud up the side of her buckskin riding pants. Even rolled up, she had managed to get them dirty. She'd have to clean them before she went home, or Grandma would be full of questions she didn't want to answer. Admitting that she had been following pirates into the swamp would surely get her put on garden duty for days—days without riding Pony or wandering with her friends.

"Well, it's probably the—"

Jukes turned back and shouted, "If you say 'crocs' one more time . . ."

"I was gonna say . . . squirrels," Jolly said. "You know, swamp squirrels."

Jukes blew air through his nostrils. "Swamp squirrels. Of all the bumble-brained nonsense . . ."

Tiger Lily popped back out once she heard their sloshy steps move away. She crept behind them for a good hundred yards before they stopped again.

"I don't even know what we're looking for," Jolly whined. "How can we find a thing when we don't know what it looks like?"

"Well, it'll look like magic," Jukes said, stumbling over his words as well as his feet. "Like, uh . . . like valuable magic. Maybe a chalice or a gemstone. Anyway, it'll be shiny in all this muck."

Jukes glanced up into the dead trees with a faraway look in his eyes. He talked about treasure the way some of the older boys talked about wild horses.

"It'll be the most beautiful thing we've ever seen. And we'll just know when we happen upon it. Everything will feel different."

"Different?" Jolly worked hard to yank his foot out of the mud. His toes were released with a thick squelch. "Who'd you hear this from, again?"

"I heard the story from Planker, who heard it from Smee, who said it came from a Lost Boy who'd overheard the fairies talking about it."

Tiger Lily winced: just their talking about her friends made her stomach ache.

"How'd he hear it from a Lost Boy? They don't like us," Jolly said, sounding hurt.

"No one likes us, you moron! We're fearsome pirates! Ain't no one friends with a pirate unless it's another pirate, and even then you gotta watch your back," Jukes said with pride, even thumping his bare chest with his fist.

"But we're friends, ain't we?" Jolly asked in a small, hopeful voice.

The tall man cleared his throat and paused, his finger on his chin as he thought of his answer. "Well . . . for now we is."

Jolly smiled. Tiger Lily rolled her eyes. Yet another

thing to add to the list of things she didn't understand about pirates. In her world, being a friend was a great honor and a solemn duty. It meant being a part of a kind of family, one you worked hard to keep safe and happy. In her world you didn't brag about being a bad friend.

"It's getting c-c-cold, doncha think?" Jolly's teeth chattered. He was sopping wet and up to his knees in chilly mud. "We been out here for a while now and we ain't even had a glimpse."

"Okay, okay. Enough for today." Jukes dropped his hands to his sides. Both of them were breathing heavily with the hard work of tromping through the mud. "We should head back. We'll leave the ship again tomorrow. Maybe even come up with an excuse to do an overnighter on land."

"Can't we just tell 'em what we're looking for?"

"No, Jolly, we cannot." Jukes was exasperated. "Do you want to share the Andon with the whole crew? Especially Hook—he'll take it for himself."

"Maybe we should. I mean, he is the captain."

Jukes scooped up a handful of slop and threw it at Jolly. It landed with a splat on the front of his shirt.

"No, we should not. All he cares about is capturing

Peter Pan. How many times has he stopped a perfectly good mission to search for that boy? How many times have we been tossed overboard or had our rations cut or worked all night on the deck looking out for that blasted boy? And for what? We're pirates!" He slapped his chest again, leaving a muddy handprint. "We hunt treasure, not flying boys! No, no. This here? This is our time to get the goods and make our fortune. Don't you want to be your own captain one day? Have your own ship?"

Jolly looked uncertain. "I don't know . . . seems like a lot of responsibility. . . ."

So, this is a mutiny, Tiger Lily thought. These pirates were acting on their own without Hook's even knowing. She wasn't sure they could pull this off in secret. She had a sudden vision of Jukes and Jolly tied together with rope, walking the plank. Below the plank, jumping out of the water like dancers, were the feared Neverland sharks. They always followed the pirates, waiting for their next meal.

"Enough," Jukes sighed, slapping his long arms against his sides. "Let's just head back for now."

Tiger Lily sprang into action, moving as quickly and quietly as she could to escape. She had to get to

Pony and across the field before these men made it out of the swamp. Even if they were headed toward the beach and she toward the fields, they were so bad at navigating, who knew where they'd end up? And she couldn't afford to be spotted. Besides, the sky was full dusk now, and she still had to find time to stop and clean up before getting back to the village.

Back on Pony, Tiger Lily made a plan to return to the beach the following evening to keep an eye on the rogue pirates. Jolly seemed bumbling enough, but Jukes was smarter and dangerous, which meant the people she loved could be at risk. First the bear and now pirates?

And for the pirates to be out on their own, without Hook? That didn't bode well for being able to predict their movements. At least with Hook you knew what you were up against, knew his limits and his moves. No, this could be the start of something very bad indeed.

She should get as much information as she could on her own. This was her chance to prove that she already had the fight to protect her friends and family. She should avoid bringing others in until she was sure of what was going on. No use in putting anyone else in harm's way. The next day she'd be better prepared.

She'd stop by Sashi's to inquire about this treasure, this Andon, before she tried Peter Pan and the Lost Boys. Just what could it be that would make these men risk the plank? And how could it be tied to the island's magic of eternal youth?

Chapter Six

The next day was warm and soft gray. The sun was never far away but refused to shine through the clouds. The bright haze made everything look like some color had run out, like when colored fabric sat out in the sun for too long. When she'd returned home the night before, Tiger Lily had washed her pants in a stream and left them hanging from her mother's clothesline all night outside her room. They were dry in the morning but a bit stiff. She took big steps and bent at the knee to try to loosen them up so she could go riding.

Gee caught her on the way to the horse stable. "Where you off to now?"

Tiger Lily sighed. She had hoped to sneak off without anyone noticing.

"Just off," she answered.

"Can I come?"

She stopped, closed her eyes, and took a deep breath. She didn't want him to think she didn't want to be around him, but she had things to do—things she wasn't ready to do with anyone else. She decided she would try to change his mind using the one thing he hated most. "I'm going out to help Sashi with her chores. We have to collect mushrooms and clean them and cut them. Then we're starting in on the wheat fields. . . ."

"You know what? You can handle that on your own," Gee answered quickly. "But maybe we can go for a ride together later?"

"Maybe," Tiger Lily replied with a smile.

Pony was waiting for her, his head held high and his nostrils flaring.

"Hey, boy. How was your night?"

He gave a soft nicker as she petted his forehead, pushing his long fine hair out of his eyes. He was a little annoyed with her, and she could tell. She'd gotten swamp muck on his white fur and given him a quick cold bath in the stream before returning him to the barn.

"Going to see Sashi before we go out on our secret mission. You ready?" He snorted and stepped backward. "Okay, okay, I get it. I'll try to keep clean today."

Finally, he whinnied and bowed his neck, granting her permission to climb onto his back. She always waited for him to allow her to climb up. It seemed rude not to. Once on top, she gave him a good scratch behind the ears before pointing him toward the far woods. And then they were off.

Sashi lived in a gnarled tree. More specifically, she lived inside a lady's handbag hanging from the tree by its handles. The bag had washed up onto the shore one day, and Tiger Lily had placed it in the tree while her excited friend watched, clapping her hands and humming a happy tune. It was a deep green velvet on the outside and faded pink silk on the inside, with wooden handles and metal clasps. Sashi had spent days stitching bright thread into the lining and hanging beads like works of art around the edges.

The best part of the bag from Tiger Lily's point of view was the design beaded on one side—all curly vines and red blooms—faded as it was. The best part from Sashi's point of view was the interior pocket, a soft, deep compartment she had made into her bed. She had even found a dull copper coin in there! She propped that coin up on a thimble (found a different day on a different shore) and then had a fine dining room table.

"Good morning," Tiger Lily sang out when she got to the base of the tree. "Is anybody home?"

There was no answer.

She cupped her hands around her mouth and called a little louder. "Good morning!"

No answer.

"Sashi, are you still sleeping?"

There was movement from the bag. It jiggled and shook, and then came a soft thud. "Ow!"

"Are you all right?"

At the top of the bag appeared a small head, curls all sticking this way and that, eyes swollen with sleep. "I would be if people wouldn't shout me awake."

She popped back inside. Tiger Lily laughed. Her friend was not an early riser. But at the same time, she hated missing anything. If Tiger Lily so much as picked a single berry without her, she'd stomp her feet and cross her arms, lamenting the missed opportunity to maybe find the perfect berry, complaining that she could have already eaten it and maybe then she wouldn't be so hungry now!

Sashi got dressed and fixed her hair, and then the two friends went to a small stream so she could wash up and clean her teeth.

Tiger Lily picked a missed piece of mud from the previous night's adventure out of Pony's mane. "Sashi, have you heard of the Andon?"

Sashi looked up quickly, suds foaming from her mouth so that her words were garbled. "And-whuuurt?"

"And-on," Tiger Lily pronounced for her. "It's supposedly some kind of treasure or something?"

Sashi rinsed and spat politely in the weeds, then wiped her face with the back of her hand. "I think I might have . . . Oh, I know! Peter mentioned it. Why?"

"I know, I heard."

Sashi looked nervous. "You heard that? Did you hear everything?"

Tiger Lily didn't want to talk about it, so she dismissed the question with a quick remark: "Stories about it are supposed to come from fairies."

"From fairies? Nah, that story came from Peter Pan." Sashi screwed up her face and tapped her chin with her finger, pondering. "I mean, Peter is the one who would know for sure. Maybe he heard it from some pirates. Who knows? Stories have a way of getting around and changing into other stories along the way. I think we should just forget all about it."

Tiger Lily thought it was odd that Sashi was so quick to change the subject, but she was also relieved; she didn't want Sashi getting involved in a dangerous mission. A bear was one thing, but pirates were entirely another. "Remember when we went hunting for the Giant of the Hilly Woods and it turned out to be just a bigger-than-average mushroom?"

"Yeah, that was a letdown." Sashi splashed water on her cheeks and rubbed them vigorously. "Okay, then, ready for the day. What are we doing today, anyway?"

"Not sure, maybe head out to Mermaid Lagoon and see if they've found anything new that's washed ashore? We could ask them about the Andon."

"You sure you want to go there?"

"Yeah, why not?" Lily was curious about yet another hesitation from her usually boisterous friend. Mermaid Lagoon was not a dangerous place.

"It's just that mermaids can be, you know . . . exhausting."

She was right. A mermaid rarely talked in a straight line, and it took a lot of effort to converse with one.

"I know they're difficult, but it's so pretty there. And

besides, we might find interesting stuff on the shore."

"Sure, let's get at it, then," Sashi said, stretching out her arms and legs, then twitching her wings into movement. "Race ya!"

Tiger Lily sighed, watching her friend zip through the trees like a colorful insect, then raced back to Pony and mounted.

"Of course you'd want to race before I'm even ready," she called out. She clicked her tongue and heels at the same time, and Pony was off, already knowing how this game went.

Deep down, she didn't really want to go to Mermaid Lagoon. The mermaids were tiresome creatures who would only demand to be entertained. It was unlikely they knew anything about the Andon, as they stayed in their own territory and weren't exactly good listeners. But Tiger Lily wanted to buy some time alone with Sashi to ask her questions casually, without raising the fairy's suspicions.

Plus, this was Neverland. . . . Who knew what could happen in a day?

Chapter Seven

The mermaids changed their names often. For a while, after they'd heard a story, they called themselves the Sirens, and they insisted it be said in a spooky voice, like "the Siiiiiireeeeeens." Once, and for many years, they were known as the Sisters, which had to be said with a certain melody so that it sounded like a fanciful announcement, like "theeeeee Sis-tahs." So Lily and Sashi weren't sure what they'd answer to that day or how to call them to the shore. Turned out they didn't have to; the maids were already out, draping their long limbs over the warm rocks that jutted out of the water, their shiny slick tails still beneath the rippled surface.

Sashi had gotten such a head start on the way there that there hadn't been time or rest enough for Tiger Lily to ask her questions about the Andon. At least she knew that it was something real, that Sashi had heard of it, that it wasn't just the fancy of daft pirates alone.

"Whew! I beat you by a mile! I've been waiting here for ages," Sashi said. She sat on a low branch, her arms behind her head as if she was relaxing. But she was still all out of breath, which let Tiger Lily know she had only just sat down. Tiger Lily smiled.

"I guess you must be bored, sitting here waiting for your slow friend, then."

Sashi couldn't lie for long. "No, not really. I just got here now. Barely made it. I could go right back to bed I'm so beat!"

Tiger Lily laughed. "Well, let's tie up Pony near some grass and go talk to these ladies."

The mermaids might have seen them already, but they were not acknowledging their existence. They liked to be courted.

Once the horse was taken care of and they'd shared some cool water from Tiger Lily's flask, the two friends made their way to the shore.

Mermaid Lagoon was beautiful, to be sure, protected

on three sides by tall cliffs of rock so pale and bare they looked like cubes of sugar. The water was shallow, so the blue shone turquoise. And bright lilies nestled among the waxy leaves that floated on the surface. There was no beach here, just a collection of smooth rocks that acted like stepping-stones from the grassy shore's edge to the largest rock, where the mermaids held court.

No one knew when the mermaids had arrived in Neverland. As far as Tiger Lily knew, they had always been there, like almost everything else. Granted, she hadn't discovered them until she was out and walking on her own, but they claimed to have shown up with the rocks.

"Only the sun and the moon were here before us," they had told her when she was little. "We are the first of firsts."

Of course, that was a whole lot of nonsense. Of anyone, Tiger Lily knew that was a lie. After all, her people had been the first. The mermaids were braggarts, and besides, that wasn't how things worked in Neverland. It seemed, from every story she could gather, that it just wasn't and then it just was.

Each mermaid in the trio was beautiful, of course;

that was the way mermaids were made. And each was unique, even though they seemed to use the same words and overlap when they spoke. The one with the iridescent orange scales had short curly hair and huge brown eyes, and she liked to sing. Her blue-scaled sister had black hair that came to her waist, just before her human torso turned to fish tail. She was a collector, and all around her were teetering piles of shiny rocks and interesting items she'd dredged up from the sandy bottom. The third had bright red scales and braided her brown hair so that it hung in ropey loops around her shoulders. Her eyes were the same shade as her scales. That could be intimidating when she got angry, which she was prone to doing when bored or challenged. These three were never apart. Tiger Lily often wondered if they grew tired of each other's company.

"You ready for this?" she whispered to Sashi.

"As ready as anyone can be to try to make sense out of fish," Sashi whispered back. Then she fit two fingers into her mouth and blew a shrill whistle, pushing the sound so hard and far that her feet lifted from the ground. The mermaid trio did not like guests showing up unannounced. They liked a moment to pose on their rock, to look as regal as possible.

Sure enough, when Tiger Lily and Sashi went into the clearing, the trio had draped over the flat rock in the center of their lagoon, their hair blowing, their limbs sparkling in the sun. None of them looked toward their visitors; each gazed off serenely, as if they had been carved from stone and placed there.

Sashi and Tiger Lily stopped at the water's edge. The fairy bent deep at the waist, bowing. She turned her head and glared at her friend until Lily mimicked her moves, bowing but keeping her eyes on the mermaids.

"Your Royal Ladyships," Sashi said in an odd accent. "It is an honor to be in your presence."

"Royal Ladyships?" Tiger Lily whispered.

"New name, just go with it."

"Yes, my . . . my Ladyships. Greetings," Tiger Lily said, stumbling over the words.

"We request permission to approach," Sashi said. She straightened up and waited for a reply.

The orange mermaid finally spoke. "You may come forth."

Tiger Lily snorted. "Is she serious?"

Again, Sashi shot her a sharp look, and when she spoke again, her teeth were clenched—a warning for

Tiger Lily to cut it out. "Much appreciated. We have some questions that only you can answer."

"It's true," the blue mermaid sighed, flipping her hair over her shoulder. "We are very wise."

"Very wise," the orange mermaid agreed.

"Indeed," the red mermaid chimed in.

"Oh my . . ." Tiger Lily caught herself before she finished, and walked alongside her more patient friend to the very edge. She hopped the first stepping-stone, then the second, and sat on the third, closest to the maids without encroaching on their perch.

"What is it you seek us out for?" Orange continued.

"My companion, the lady Tiger Lily, has need of your . . . uh . . . smartiness."

"About something called the Andon," added Tiger Lily.

"With the right gift, she shall be given our smartiness about this Andon," Blue replied.

"Ooooh," Red said, clapping, "I love gifts!"

"Gifts?" Tiger Lily looked at her empty hands. "No one said anything about bringing a gift," she hissed to the fairy.

"Well, think of something if you want them to talk."

She patted her shirt and her pants. Nothing. There

was a small knife belted to her side, but there was no way she was handing that over to these talking fish. She ran her hands through her hair and checked her wrists—nothing. Why was she even bothering to look? The mermaids were not known for their "smartiness," just their exceptional gossiping skills.

Then she had an idea. She lifted the bottom hem of her shirt, pulled her knife sheath off her belt, and took out the blade.

Sashi looked alarmed. "You're not giving them that, are you?"

Tiger Lily placed the knife on the rock beside her and made a big show of holding up the now empty leather sheath in front of her. The mermaids had dropped the aloof-royalty act and watched her every move now that a gift was potentially in the works.

"In this case, I have a very special magic, one that was given to me by my great-great-great-great-grandfather." She spoke in a loud, clear voice, still displaying the sheath as if it held this magic thing she had just made up. "To get it, he himself wrestled a white bear, who had stolen it from a giant bird, who had pecked the skull in Skull Island out of sheer rock."

"What are you saying?" Sashi whispered. "There is no way anyone would believe—"

"Oooooh," Red cooed. "I love magic, and white bears."

"What is it?" Blue leaned on her elbows to get closer to the edge of their rock, pushing Orange aside to get a better look.

"It is"—Tiger Lily faltered for a moment before deciding on the answer—"eternal beauty!"

She thrust her arms straight out and held the sheath like an offering for the sky.

Now, the idea of the mermaids' being interested in eternal beauty was kind of ridiculous. For one thing, they didn't age, so eternity was easy. For another, they were already so beautiful it was hard to choose which one was the most beautiful. What use could they possibly have for such a thing?

"Ahhhhh, what?" Sashi cried. Tiger Lily shrugged a bit. The pair waited for a response, and at first there was none. The sisters sat there, their eyes glued to the sheath.

And then . . .

"*Oooooh! I love eternal beauty!*" Red was clapping, bouncing the bottom half of her body in the water. "I want it!"

"Me too! I want it, too!" Blue was quick to join in, trying to be louder than Red.

Tiger Lily and Sashi sighed. It had worked! Lily lowered the sheath and looked inside. "Yup, eternal beauty. Beauty for . . . uh . . . all time. Beauty that can never be lost . . . ever."

"Wait," Orange boomed, holding out her hand to stop her sisters, who had begun to argue. "We need to choose who the recipient will be, and I propose, since I was the first to speak, that I should get it."

Blue was quick to jump in. "But I was the one who asked for the gift! It's mine!"

"I called it first!" Red was pouting before she finished speaking.

Seeing they were getting nowhere fast, and not wanting this to turn into an all-out argument over a made-up gift, Tiger Lily spoke up. "Silence, Your Ladyships. There is enough eternal beauty for all three of you."

"Yes!" Red turned in a neat little circle so that the water was set into a swirl. Then she became very still, her eyes narrowed. "You're sure it will work? We don't like to be disappointed."

"Yes," Blue agreed. "A pirate came by once before—a

handsome pirate, too. He came with promises of jewels for us if we showed him how to swim."

"And he never brought us jewels," Orange said, remembering. They all nodded slowly, in an eerie kind of synchronicity.

"Wh-what happened? To the pirate?" Tiger Lily was almost afraid to ask.

"We swam alongside the *Jolly Roger* and sang loudly outside his window every night until he changed his mind," Blue mused. "We got our gift in the end."

Tiger Lily swallowed hard. From the corner of her eye she saw Sashi shudder. But she had come this far. She didn't want to think of what might happen if they tried to walk away now without this eternal beauty bestowed as promised. "So, I will ask my trusty companion, the, uh, lady Sashi, to take this container and sprinkle the gift over you, an equal amount for each maiden."

She passed the sheath to the fairy, who gave her a puzzled look before hefting the weight of an item almost the same size as her.

"Lady Sashi, the eternal beauty will come out like *pixie dust*, so careful not to spill it." She said *pixie dust* in a deliberate, slow way, raising an eyebrow.

"Oooh." Sashi caught on. "Yes, I have seen such magic before, Lady Lily. I will be very careful."

She shifted the sheath so that it rested on her shoulder, and slowly flew over the water, above the mermaids. They giggled and clasped their hands, waiting.

"Okay then, ready?"

"Ready," the mermaids replied in unison. They could barely contain their excitement.

Sashi paused. "Uh, maybe you'd better close your eyes. You don't want to get any of the beauty in your eye. It could sting."

They quickly shut their eyes tight.

"Hurry! I want the beauty now and forever," Orange called out.

"Okay, here it comes," Sashi sang out.

Sashi tipped over the empty sheath, but of course, nothing came out. Instead, she wiggled and jiggled and shook out her wings until a sprinkling of pixie dust fell from the sky, over each of the mermaids waiting below.

"I can feel it!" Blue tilted her face up to catch every drop. "I can feel myself getting more beautiful!"

"Me too!" the other two chorused.

"There. It is bestowed upon you," Sashi said.

She huffed and puffed, carrying the sheath back to

Tiger Lily, who grabbed it from her and mouthed a quick *thank you*.

Each mermaid opened her eyes and gazed upon her sisters, then regarded her own face in the reflective water while the 'gift bringers' waited with bated breath. A long moment of silence, and then . . .

"Oh, joy! We are even more beautiful than before!" Red said, ecstatic.

Blue touched her cheeks, ran her hands up and down her arms. "We are miraculous!"

Orange turned and clicked her tongue at Tiger Lily and Sashi. "Oh, you poor dears. You must feel so plain and ordinary now—even more so than before."

Sashi was about to retort, but Tiger Lily spoke up. "We do indeed. Now, if we could get our answers about the Andon, we'll be out of your luxurious hair quick enough. Then you can get back to your day of . . . uh, being miraculous."

She had been betting on the mermaids' famous vanity to get through this. They believed they were the prettiest things in the whole world. When Tiger Lily had complained to her grandmother about their bragging, the Elder had replied, "It's good to love yourself. Loving yourself shows you're grateful for life and means you can show others the way you are to be valued. But making others feel bad because of it, well, that's when it's a problem. You must always be kind with love."

When they were finally done complimenting themselves and each other, they returned to posing on their rock, more regal than before.

"The Andon, yes, we have heard of this," Orange began, speaking slower than was necessary, to seem important. "It used to be spoken of more often. It's been a long time—"

"The longest time," Red interjected.

"Which usually means it's not around anymore." Orange examined her hands, admiring the shape of her fingers. "We know everything of any value around here, and we haven't heard anything new. I'm sure Peter Pan would've told us about it, too."

Tiger Lily jumped at this. "Wait, what do you mean 'not around anymore'? Where would it have gone?"

But it was too late. The mermaids became distracted again.

"Oh, I love when Peter tells us stories," Blue said. "He tells the best stories."

"He tells them to me most of all," Orange spat.

"No way. He only really comes here to tell me stories.

You two just happen to be here, that's all," Red said, patting her hair.

"You take that back! He comes for me!" Orange turned on her sister.

Tiger Lily could not stand all this vain arguing, and she certainly could not understand squabbling with your sisters, especially over a boy. Peter Pan was her friend, but still.

"Ladies! Ladies!" She clapped her hands and spoke loudly. "Where do you think the Andon would have gone if it's not here anymore?"

"Where does anything go? Washed away. . . . Crocodile ate it . . ." Blue began.

"Pirates stole it. . . . Lost Boys smashed it. . . . Birds carried it away . . ." Red finished.

"Okay, but you don't know that for sure," Tiger Lily stated. "And birds? What is it that birds could carry away? Is it small?"

"I suppose. But also, I think it's quite large." Orange lay on her back now, floating a slow circle around the rock.

"What does that even mean?" Tiger Lily was getting annoyed, and she had a lot of patience, so that was really saying something. Then she had a thought. "Wait. You haven't seen the Andon, have you?"

The mermaids were silent, maybe even pretending they couldn't hear her.

"I'm right, aren't I? You've never seen it. And . . . Why is it called the Andon?"

"It is the most valuable thing in Neverland," Blue replied. "And it's named after a brave mermaid—my very sister, in fact—who swam away one day and hasn't been seen since."

"Did she take it?"

"No one has taken it, or we would have heard about it. We hear everything," Red continued. "Also," she said, turning to Blue, "Andon was *my* sister."

"She was more my sister than either of yours," Orange shouted.

"So it . . ." Tiger Lily interrupted, not bothering to explain that if the mermaids were sisters, then any sister of one would be sister to all. "It could be anything, look like anything, but you don't know what it is, and no one you know has seen it, but also you know for sure that it is still around?"

Red lowered her head on her folded arms. "I'm

bored now." She sighed, then sat up with a start. "I know! Let's go show the dolphins our new beauty!"

"Oh, how lucky the dolphins are today," Blue said.

"I can't wait to see their little eyes pop out," Orange said, laughing.

There was nothing, apparently, like shared narcissism to make the mermaids forget about their tiffs.

Before Tiger Lily or Sashi could get another word out, the mermaids were underwater, swimming fast and hard away from them.

"Well," the fairy said, crossing her arms over her chest and hovering near her friend's side, "there go the very beautiful, very annoying ladyships."

"And any hope of learning about the Andon," Tiger Lily added.

"Oh, I don't know," the fairy replied, flying alongside the girl as she carefully made her way over the rocks to the shore. "They are not exactly reliable, you know. They'd rather comb their hair and talk about a silly boy who uses fairy magic as his own than get their stories straight."

Tiger Lily did know one thing, though: if she wanted to beat the pirates to the Andon, she needed to make a new plan.

Chapter Eight

"I'm exhausted." Sashi touched down on Pony's mane and made her way to Tiger Lily's shoulder, then sat beside her friend's ear and wrapped her hand in a tendril of her hair in case she should lose balance. "Talking to mermaids is just . . ."

"Exhausting?" Tiger Lily offered.

"The worst," Sashi finished. "And you didn't even get any real intel. Should have known we were in for nothing more than a song-and-dance routine."

"Yes, it was a waste of time," Tiger Lily said, unable to hide her disappointment.

"At least we got to see the great and sacred magic of 'eternal beauty.'"

They both laughed.

"Yes, it wasn't my best work, but it did the trick."

"'Trick' is right." Sashi wiped a tear her laughter had squeezed from her eye. "Well, I mean, we did learn some things."

"Like what?"

"Well, the mermaids will fall for anything. And also, the mermaids have no idea what the Andon is, which, judging by the way they gobble up information and hearsay, means either it's not real and they made it up, or it is real and no one is talking about it."

"I suppose. But still . . ." She sighed.

Hearing the sadness in her friend's voice, Sashi got brighter, more positive. "Bah! Those mermaids, they don't know that much. They can't even keep their names for longer than it takes the tides to turn. Never mind about them. Just forget we even went there."

"We'll need to talk to someone else," said Tiger Lily. "And Peter did mention the Andon. . . ."

"Why does it always have to be Peter?" Sashi folded her arms across her chest. "He's just a boy, after all."

"I know," Tiger Lily said. "But he's a boy who has had a lot of adventures, and so he knows a lot."

She was frustrated that she would have to go to

Peter. She had really wanted to figure this out on her own. And a part of her wanted there to be a treasure, maybe even the kind of treasure you had to find with a map. The Lost Boys were always going on and on about treasure maps. They sounded fun.

They rode Pony out of the lagoon and into the fields in silence. The sky was still gray, and a slight wind had put a chill in the air. That meant swimming was probably out, at least until the clouds cleared.

"You'd think they'd be all gobsmacked having an actual flying fairy there." Sashi was still sore about the whole Pan business. "Instead, they went all moon-eyed about Peter and his assisted magic. *Pfft.* Amateur."

Tiger Lily had known that was coming. "Well, I, for one, am aware that the fairies do all the heavy lifting in that situation. Literally," she said.

Sashi was pleased by her answer. "So, whatcha wanna do now?"

All Tiger Lily wanted to do was solve the riddle of the Andon, but it was obvious her friend did not.

"Maybe you should go take a nap. Maybe I will, too." It was a fib. There was no way she could sleep now, but she thought maybe this would buy her some time to plan, alone.

Sashi tap-danced across her shoulder, giggling. "No way! It's early. Let's make a game to play. Oh! How about a race game?"

"Ugh, why does it always have to be a racing game? Can't you just stay still?"

The fairy bent her knees and launched off her friend, spinning neat pirouettes in the air. "Because you need to move. I can see it." She flew close to Tiger Lily's face, peering into one eye, then the other. "It's right there." She tapped her forehead.

Tiger Lily shooed her away. "Get out of here! What do you even mean?"

Hovering, Sashi crossed her arms over her chest. "We've known each other a long time, Lily. I can see when something's bothering you. And when something is bothering you, you need to move. It's always been that way."

Tiger Lily got shy all of a sudden. "You . . . you see that?"

Her friend punched her lightly on the arm. It felt like a slight tickle.

"Of course, you giraffe! I know you. And I also know when you need some room to make all those moves. Just thought I'd try to help is all."

She flew circles around Pony, shifting her body to make the bells on her dress sing. "When you were shorter, you used to sneak away from your grandma and run round. Not far, because you knew you'd worry her, so just like around and around the village, or the fishing rocks, or the forest, wherever she'd taken you. It was usually when you had something on your mind, something you were trying to figure out. You'd rather run than talk. But that was before you got Pony."

Sashi laughed at the memory of pint-sized Tiger Lily, her little legs pumping as hard as they could. Then she settled down and took long, whooshing strides with the wind. "Is this why you're looking for the Everstill? Because you've got something on your mind?"

Lily scrunched her nose. "You mean the Andon?"

"You seem like you're looking for a distraction." Sashi was good at figuring out her best friend. She frowned. "Tiger Lily, are you searching because Peter mentioned the Andon the other night?"

She didn't want to admit that Peter's words about her needing more fight had gotten to her. But of course, that wasn't the only reason. Tiger Lily cleared her throat, tipped her chin toward her chest, and mumbled an answer. "No, it was . . ."

"What's that?" Sashi zoomed in closer, a hand cupped around her ear.

The girl coughed and spoke a bit louder, embarrassed by her answer. "Pirates."

"Pirates!" Sashi screamed, jumping back as if the air were solid ground.

"Don't be yelling that out loud! Yes, pirates, two of them. They were on their own, planning and searching."

Tiger Lily told the fairy about Bill Jukes and Jolly, the way they had come in on a boat without Hook, and how their mission to find the most valuable treasure in all Neverland was a secret from the fearsome captain. She told her about how they'd heard of it from a long list of people, including a Lost Boy, and how they planned to come back the next day.

Sashi listened in silence, not even asking a million questions like she usually did.

Saying all of this out loud made Tiger Lily even more curious, more determined to figure it out.

"You're going out to follow them again?" Sashi finally asked, without a hint of teasing. She must have thought it was at least worth wondering about.

Tiger Lily noticed her friend's tone had changed. That her best friend wasn't blowing it off was even more proof that the Andon could exist and that it might need to be rescued from the likes of Hook's men. "Not sure."

"It sounds dangerous, Lil," she added. "I don't know that you should be getting mixed up in this. Wasn't that incident with the bear the other night scary enough? We're not strong enough to face a danger like this."

She wasn't wrong, and Tiger Lily knew it. What would she do if she was found out? Or if they managed to find the treasure and she cornered them? After all, there were two of them and only one of her.

She said what she was sure she was supposed to say, even if it felt like it might not be true. "No, I won't follow them again. That would be silly, right?"

The girls said their farewells, and Tiger Lily watched as Sashi took the long way back to her purse home, zipping low to run her hands over the tops of tall grass and following a pack of velvety butterflies when they pumped their wings down to the shoreline. Tiger Lily envied the fairy. She looked so happy, so carefree flying off.

Suddenly, she felt a flash of anger that she had to even think about things like growing up and having to protect her family and Sashi and the Lost Boys. If you listened to Peter Pan, you'd think growing up was the worst thing that could happen. He vowed to stay a boy forever and made the Lost Boys make the same promise. But then again, Peter was alone except for those boys. He didn't have a whole community counting on him or holding him up, making everything better and brighter.

It didn't seem fair that Peter was the only one she was certain knew more about the Andon. Maybe it was for the best he'd gone off to London, because she wanted to find the Andon on her own, without his help, and see for herself if she needed it.

But she wasn't strong enough yet; that was certain. Thinking about her village, Tiger Lily decided she would go out one last time to spy on the pirates. Andon or not, at the very least she wanted to make sure they weren't getting any closer to her home or causing any harm. If they were, she'd turn to her grandmother and the others to see what should be done about it.

She waited until the fairy disappeared over the rose patch, its thorny vines impossible to penetrate; then she turned Pony toward the shore so she could wait for the two bumbling pirates to return.

A part of her felt bad for lying, for going off on

this adventure alone once again, but these were pirates, after all, and she didn't want to put anyone else at risk. Plus, there was a part of her that felt silly for chasing a treasure that might only be a story. Still, if it was true, Tiger Lily could finally prove herself—and maybe the adventure would help her make a decision about growing up.

Chapter Nine

The pirates came earlier than before. The sun was still nestled near the top of the sky, hiding its brightest shine behind moody cotton clouds, when she saw them approach. They looked just as dirty as the day before, with a few new additions. The mud from the swamp striped their cheeks and foreheads.

"Okay, boy, you know the drill; you stay here," Tiger Lily told Pony. "I'll come get you as soon as I can."

She climbed down and walked the horse to a semicircle of bushes heavy with bright pink berries sticky with sweet juice.

"And don't eat too many," Lily chided him, plucking

a pinch berry and feeding it to him. "You know you get a sore stomach when you don't have control."

Pony snorted, shaking his head one way, then the other.

"Yeah, yeah, wise guy. We'll see who's being all lippy when he's up all night with a gassy belly."

She patted his snout and crouched low to creep back to the beach. He paid her no mind, already rooting around and taking big mouthfuls of sweet fruit straight off the branches.

Jukes sat in the bow, swiping a long spyglass left and then right, twisting the barrel to focus and refocus. Every now and then, he turned and checked the blue expanse behind them. So far they were not being followed. But judging by the way he twitched and turned, she could tell Jukes thought that might change at a moment's notice. This meant they were still acting in secret.

They were clumsy bringing the boat ashore, splashing and stumbling all the way. This time they went away from the swamp, heading into the flower fields.

The blooms there were delicate and smelled like the best meal and the sweetest breeze and the top of a baby's head all at once: bright blue bella knots, lush red pop-pops, lacy yellow sundrils that turned to follow their namesake as it moved across the sky. The blooms grew huge and vibrant for a season before dropping off like colorful rain so that new blooms could form. Because of this fragile beauty, people usually avoided crushing the pulpy stems and powder-dusted petals. But Bill Jukes and Jolly tromped straight through, carelessly, like rolling boulders.

Where she hid, Tiger Lily winced. This land was more than a place to live; it was a home to protect, and even the loss of flowers was something to mourn. She thought she would come back to the field and collect the lost blooms, then take them back to the village so her aunts could use what was possible in their medicines. At least then it wouldn't be a total loss.

To follow the pirates, Tiger Lily had no choice but to step in the carnage of crumpled flowers, though she stepped as lightly as possible. "Sorry, sorry. So sorry. Sorry!"

The dirty duo had stopped just ahead, having reached the top of an incline at the far end of the field. Tiger Lily knew this spot. The ground was loose in places, so one had to step carefully and go down in a kind of zigzag to slow the descent. They stood arguing at the top. Tiger Lily dropped to her belly to wait.

"G'won, then," Jukes shouted, his voice echoing.

"You sure?"

"Yes, yeah, I'm sure, all right? Just go!" Jukes clapped his companion on the back. It was more of a push, really, and Jolly lurched forward and then disappeared.

After a moment, and with one last look back, the taller man followed.

Tiger Lily advanced, almost at the precipice of the cliff, when she heard them yelling and carrying on. And she knew why even before she looked over the edge. She knew what had happened—what always happened when one wasn't careful on this hill. She crept to the edge and peered over.

Sure enough, there they were, crumpled in a heap of old clothes and dirty limbs, one on top of the other, at the bottom of the incline. Tiger Lily covered her mouth to keep from laughing out loud. They were writhing and groaning and trying to untangle themselves.

"Jukesy, come on, now. Get yer elbow out of my mouth."

"Get yer trap offa my elbow!"

Jolly had taken the worst of it, having landed hard on the rocky ground, directly underneath the hulking

Jukes. He sounded winded, his voice coming out small and in wheezes.

As they sorted themselves out, stood, rearranged clothing, and found Jukes's boots, Tiger Lily stealthily lowered herself down the bank on the far side and climbed into the thick bottom branches of a gnarled oak—the perfect high vantage point. Every now and then there was a loud snap, like lightning hitting the trees. Soon she realized the noise was Bill Jukes tearing thick branches off and breaking them in two; in his massive hands, they were like twigs. All of a sudden, they stopped being so funny. She realized the danger posed by a temper in a man that size.

Tiger Lily almost fell asleep in that tree, watching them closely while the wind grew calm and the sun came out for one last shine before pulling itself toward bed. She could see from up high that the men were going in circles, but quickly realized that they had no idea. They were lost on solid ground, with no sense of direction or strategy.

Finally, they returned to the cliff.

"If we ain't there for dinner slop, I'm eatin' your mattress," Jukes yelled at Jolly, who was trailing behind him.

"If we ain't there for dinner, I'm eatin' me own mattress," Jolly replied.

Tiger Lily heard her own belly rumble in response, and she rubbed at it, trying not to think about the good food that would be waiting for her when she got home. She grew tense when the men stopped directly below where she lay, her belly flat on the branch, her breath shallow and quiet. Jolly collapsed on the ground, and Jukes leaned his massive weight against the trunk she had climbed.

"Can't do the hill just yet, mate. Need to catch my breath," said Jukes.

He did seem exhausted. His head hung as if it were too heavy for his neck. His back was curved in like a question mark.

"Okay, I'll wait for ya, then," Jolly replied, as if he were doing him a favor. Truth was he was so red in the face it was amazing he was still breathing.

"You know, I've been thinkin'," Jukes began.

"Congratulations!" Jolly said without a hint of sarcasm, as if truly proud of his companion's intellectual skills. "I always knew you was a scholar."

Jukes sighed, so deeply he closed his eyes, and placed his fingers to pinch the top of his nose, as if his head suddenly hurt. "Anyway, I was thinking maybe we're doing this all wrong like. Maybe we need to find our mast man."

"Mast man? Whatcha mean? You wanna bring another crewman in on the job?"

"No, you bobbin. I don't mean another pirate. I mean a mast man. Like how on our ship the mast man knows what he's lookin' for and he stands up top and watches for it? Guides us, like?"

"Sure, sure. Like when Smee is mast man and Hook straps him up in the crow's nest to look for rocks that could poke holes in the boat?"

"Well, that's more of a Hook punishment." He chuckled at a memory. "But yeah. Yeah, exactly like that." He rubbed his chin, which only left more streaks of mud in his beard. "We need someone who knows what it is we seek and can call it out, see?"

"But who knows, Jukesy, other than us two?"

"Well, let's track where we know it from. Planker and Smee know." He extended a finger with each name, as if he was counting. "And they's out. No more pirates. Smee heard it from one of those Lost Boys, who picked it up from fairy gossip."

"Ah! So we grab one of those kids up, then?"

"Looks like, Jolly, looks like."

In the tree, Tiger Lily held her breath. They were going after the Lost Boys? But they were just kids! Wild, troublesome, dangerous little creatures, but kids nonetheless. Her heart beat quick and hard.

"First things first: we get up that hill, we row back to ship, then tomorrow we start asking around all sneaky like to see who knows where those brats live."

And then they were off. Tiger Lily followed at a safe distance, ran back to Pony, and watched as they rowed out to the horizon. She stayed there longer than she needed to, making sure they didn't double back. When the moon started to stretch into the corners of the evening, she took off at a mad gallop to make it home, knowing she had at least until the next day to warn her friends.

Suddenly, this didn't seem like such a fun game— not now, when there was so much more than treasure at stake.

Chapter
Ten

She woke up bright and early the next morning, but later than she'd wanted. All the anxiety from the night before meant sleep had refused to settle in. She'd been up tossing and turning and deciding what the right thing to do was. It wasn't until she had decided to talk to her grandmother that she was able to drift off.

She dressed quickly and burst out her door. She'd made up her mind, and she had to find Grandma right away. She would feel much better once Grandma knew, once she had taken the burden off Tiger Lily.

She hadn't gotten past her front garden before she knew something was different. It was too quiet. None of her aunties were working in the yard. The lines set up between the trees were empty; no one was doing any wash. And the fire hadn't been lit. She walked to the pit and pushed around the wood with her toe. It was old and cool to the touch. It hadn't been going since the previous night at the latest.

She wandered out to the walkway that connected the different households. There were no fires anywhere, no aunties in any yard.

Panic flooded her brain, and when it reached her feet, she began to run. She went to her neighbors', but no one was home, then the next and the next. No one. Finally, at the fifth structure, she found a boy, stacking wood.

"Neilie, nephew, where is everyone?" She was frantic. Her tone scared him, and he dropped the kindling he carried. He looked like a boy who had been up to mischief at some point and was waiting to get caught for it. Tiger Lily recognized that look, because she had gotten up to enough mischief in her younger days. She supposed, in a way, she still did.

"They went out to fish." He said it slowly, as if she were unable to understand. When she didn't respond right away, he used one hand to mimic the swimming of a fish.

The same fishing trip she had been excused from, for years . . .

"Oh, no! That started today?" She bent over and put her hands on her knees, catching her breath and slowing her heart and her thoughts.

"Uh-huh. Just some Elders and some kids are left." He approached her and put a small hand on her shoulder. "Only two hunters stayed behind in the village. You okay, Lily?"

She was touched by his concern. She put a hand on his cheek. "Yes, nephew, I'm fine. I just forgot is all. Wait . . . hunters? Where are they? Are there any still here?"

She could still rally the hunters to come with her. They could ride out with her and warn the Lost Boys, or convince them to come back to the village with them. Or maybe even fight off the pirates if they had already found them.

"Gone."

"Gone where?"

He lifted his arms and shrugged. "Hunting, probably.

They said they were going to go out, but I'm not sure when they'll be back."

Tiger Lily stood there for another moment, her hands on her knees, while the small child rubbed her back.

"You don't look so good," he cooed, probably mimicking the voice his mother used when he was sick. "You want some water?"

She shook her head. Then she collected herself, planted a kiss on the boy's head, and went back to her own place.

One thing was for sure: she had to get to the Lost Boys before the pirates did.

Pony was lying down in the meadow when she arrived.

She whistled. "Come on, boy. We have to get going."

He looked at her with bashful, sleepy eyes but didn't move. He just swished his tail.

She whistled again. "Pony, come on, boy. It could be an emergency." She clapped her hand against her thigh, trying to call him to her.

Still, Pony just lay there. He did give her one long whinny and twitched his neck a little.

"Oh, no. You did it, didn't you? You ate too many pinch berries? Po-ny, I warned you."

He nickered and looked away, ashamed.

"*Aaaargh!*" She spun in a circle, frustrated. She didn't want to drag Pony out when he wasn't feeling well, even if he had done it to himself. Besides, he couldn't run very fast in this condition. What was she to do? She had to get to the Lost Boys before the pirates did.

"Wait a minute. . . ." She put two fingers into her mouth and whistled long and sharp, then waited.

Pony was ignoring her, but from the back of the field came a rustling of leaves. She whistled a second time and waited again.

Finally, a black horse with white spots near its hind legs wandered across the field. She seemed old, and she walked slowly, carefully choosing her steps. But her head was held straight, and her eyes were good. She spotted Tiger Lily right away and approached her.

"Ah, there you are, girl. Sorry to disturb you." Tiger Lily reached out, and the mare put her long head in the girl's hands. Tiger Lily petted her snout and ran her fingers along her silky dark mane. "It's just me. Grandma is off fishing. But I need you."

She knew her grandmother wouldn't mind her taking her horse out. Grandma rarely ran her these days, and the horse had settled into a quiet life, enjoying the freshwater stream at the back of the field and spending time with a family of chickens that lived back there and provided eggs for the community.

"May I ask something of you?" Tiger Lily whispered close to her ear. "I need to go out to save my friends. Can you take me there?"

The horse closed her eyes, as if considering, then lowered herself, bending her strong neck, granting permission.

"Thanks, girl."

Tiger Lily swung herself up onto the horse, feeling the strength in her body after all this time. She was solid, built wide and sturdy, but still soft and beautiful. In so many ways, this horse's temperament reminded her of her grandmother's—the same patient demeanor, the same generosity of spirit. They were a perfect match, rider and horse. Tiger Lily looked at her own Pony, impetuous, stubborn, but loyal and brave—fast, too—and thought they were also a perfect match. She thought of the *Jolly Roger*, the stinky, scary, snarly boat the pirates rode. Even them: they, too, were a match. She supposed you could learn a lot by paying attention to the things people surrounded themselves with when they had a choice.

"You rest up, bubble belly. And make sure you drink lots of water," she called out to Pony. He lowered his head to the soft grass and sighed. She could hear his stomach squeaking and churning from where she was. Then she was off.

"It's the Lost Boys," she instructed the mare. "As quick as you can. Pirates are looking for them."

At the word *pirates*, the mare's ears pricked up and her gait quickened. Soon they were galloping down the path, bursting out into the open, and moving fast toward the woods.

Chapter Eleven

Sometimes the Lost Boys spent their days at what they called Fort Fierce, a tree house they'd assembled out of old branches and wood washed up from shipwrecks. It was not safe by any measure and leaned dangerously out of the tree, every wall nailed down at an odd angle. When Peter Pan wasn't around, some of them liked to go there to eat their meals, play their games, and dream their dreams.

The day they'd finished construction, Curly looked up at the crooked structure and said, not unkindly, "Looks like you, Nibs."

Nibs smiled real big, his cheeks pink. "It's great," he

declared. "Professional-like work, chaps!" They had all cheered, clapping each other on the back.

When Tiger Lily reached the fort and dismounted, she found the ground was littered with the debris of wild children: a broken bow, one shoe (the sole covered in holes), a long and tattered swatch of red fabric, a pile of round rocks, and too many apple cores to count.

"Hello? Is anyone here? Curly? Nibs?"

She called out for them and waited for a response, carefully stepping around the debris. As messy as it was, she had seen it worse. They were slowly getting better. Of course, that might change when Peter Pan got back and riled them up into full Lost Boys mode—all adventure, no cares.

"Twins? You here?"

No one answered, and she felt the first prickles of panic in the backs of her knees.

"Lost Boys? If you're here, answer me!"

No answer. But . . . there was no noise at all, not a bird chirping or a squirrel chittering at her from a branch. And if the animals were gone, that usually meant there were people around.

"Come on, I'm serious," she sighed, making her way

to the base of the tree that held Fort Fierce. "Answer me now!"

There was a small sound, maybe a giggle, high above her.

She rolled her eyes. *Oh, these scoundrels.* "Come on. I don't have time for a game right now."

"Neither do we," Nibs called down. He couldn't contain his excitement anymore. "Curly's training crows up here! Come see!"

Just then a black bird burst out the small window, cawing, and took to the sky.

"Aw, come on back, Flappy. We got more training to do!" Curly's head popped out as she watched the bird leave. A splat of poop landed on the sill, dangerously close to the girl's face. "That's not very gentlemanly of you!" She shook her fist at the sky, then turned to look at Tiger Lily. "Hey, Lily. I'm working with birds now. Gonna have our own army, we are."

Tiger Lily shook her head. "That's great, but this is serious. There are pirates after you!"

A small head peeked out from a broken slat in the front wall of the fort. "Pirates?"

It was Twin One. "Real pirates?"

She seemed more excited than scared. Typical Lost Boys reaction.

"Yes, One. Real pirates. Grab whoever else is up there and get down here now." She paced the perimeter of the clearing, waiting for them, all long limbs and clumsy feet, to clamber down the trunk. It was the same quartet that had joined them for the game of feetball only days before. Among the Lost Boys, they particularly liked to stick together. They talked excitedly to each other as they descended.

"Pirates! Bet it's Hook!"

"I'll kick him in the legs! I'll kick him till he can't move."

"Must have heard about our skills. Probably want us to join them."

"We're more piratey than the pirates! They probably want to join us."

Finally, they were on the ground and immediately started asking questions: Who was coming? When were they coming? How many? Did they have time to gather their slingshots and arrows? Tiger Lily held both hands in front of her, motioning for them to stop. They kicked and spun and shouted for a few more minutes before settling into silence.

"Listen . . . listen. There are two pirates on our shores looking for a treasure. . . ."

This set them all atwitter again. Tiger Lily squeezed her eyes shut, trying to hold on to her temper. Usually, she had more patience for this lot, but not now—not when they were in danger.

"*Hey!* I said *listen!*"

Not used to hearing her yell, they shut their mouths tight. The twins sat hard on the ground, as if she were a teacher they had to obey. They had never been to a school—or at least didn't remember attending one—but were fascinated by stories about it. Sometimes Tiger Lily came here to teach them the things she learned from the Elders—science, gardening, and spelling—and they insisted she pretend they were in a classroom.

"The pirates—Bill Jukes and Jolly—have been here the last two days, as far as I can tell, and are looking for something called the Andon." She paused here and scanned the children's faces. Not a flicker of recognition, not a twitch. Just Twin Two scratching her nose, dangerously close to picking it.

"And they seem to think that you all can tell them where it is." She paced back and forth in front of the motley lineup. "Now, do any of you know where this Andon is?"

They all shook their heads.

"No one has spoken to the pirates about this treasure? Maybe made something up to send them on a wild-goose chase, just for jokes? Or Peter? I know he's heard of it."

Again they shook their heads.

"And we're sure we have no idea what it could be?"

Once more, they indicated they did not.

She stopped pacing, crossed her arms over her chest, and tapped her foot. Well, this was a mystery. It wasn't unusual for stories to get confused. People liked to tell them, but not many bothered to get them right, too excited to tell their own versions and be known as good storytellers above all. What was she to do now?

"Why'd they think we know?" Curly asked, always the spokesperson for this crew. She often became the unofficial official leader when Peter wasn't about, and it was a job she took seriously. She liked to dress to indicate this status. That day she had twigs that resembled a small set of buck's horns pushed into her hair. "How'd you even know?"

Tiger Lily paused. She hated to be a bad example,

especially to this impressionable lot, but she didn't have time to choose her words more carefully. "Because I was following them and overheard them."

"Following pirates? Of course you did." Curly snapped her fingers, quickly and sharply. The others began to mimic her, so that Tiger Lily was surrounded by a quiet applause. "You're a world-class adventurer, Lily!"

"No, I took a big risk. Never get too close to pirates." She did feel a twinge of pride but covered it up quick. She didn't want to encourage them to be reckless. "And pay attention," she said, covering her sudden shame with a quick flash of anger. "They said one of their men heard from a Lost Boy who'd heard it from fairies that the Andon was the most valuable thing in Neverland, and they plan to steal it."

"Which pirate said that?" Nibs was already trying to piece it together. He liked a good mystery. Sometimes he organized scavenger hunts across Neverland for his friends, giving cryptic clues and coming up with detailed backstories. "And which Lost Boy told him? Maybe it was one of the others. We could ask them when they get back from campin' out, maybe."

"Didn't say," she admitted. "But they said they were

coming to get the information direct like. From the source itself."

Nibs rubbed his chin and began pacing, just as Tiger Lily had been doing. "So, they want to hear the information straight from the horse's mouth, eh?" He looked over quickly at her grandmother's mare. "No offense."

The mare nickered a low response. She didn't pay much attention to these wild children and instead used the time to fill up on the tall grass that grew here.

"That's right." Tiger Lily kept scanning the edge of the forest, looking for any movement in the trees.

"So if that's the case, that they want to get to the original tellers, why would they come here for us?" Curly asked.

Tiger Lily raised her eyebrows at her. "What do you mean?"

"Well," she continued, "if they are coming for the original informants, wouldn't that mean they would be going to the fairies?" She ended with her hands up in a questioning shrug. "You said they said the one who told them was a Lost Boy who was told by the fairies. We're not the first in the chain—more like the middlemen."

No one said anything. They turned their eyes toward Tiger Lily, now still and thinking. She was frozen, her hands on her hips, looking at Curly, who was starting to get worried.

"Uh, Tiger Lily? Are you still with us?"

"Oh." Her mouth was perfectly round. "Oh, no . . ."

The fairies! Why hadn't she thought of it? She assumed they'd meant the Lost Boys when they had said *kids*, but it was the fairies who were supposed to have been the first to tell of the treasure.

"Oh, noooo!" And then she was off, dashing across the clearing, kicking apple cores as she rushed. She pulled herself up on the horse in one fluid movement and turned back into the woods. She was long gone before the Lost Boys even had a chance to gather their thoughts.

"Well," Twin Two said, "that was weird."

Nibs took a step, bent down to pick up the broken arrow at his feet, and raised both hands above his head. "That was . . . magnificent! We need to hang out with Tiger Lily more." He was excited by all the adrenaline and intrigue.

"'Cept she always makes us clean our clothes," Twin One said, wrinkling her nose.

"And brush our teeth," Twin Two said, sticking her tongue out.

"Well, yeah," Nibs conceded. "There is always a downside to fun."

Soon enough they were back up in Fort Fierce, having carried up most of the pile of rocks for their slingshots. Now they were on the lookout for treasure-seeking pirates, just in case they decided to show up after all. They could always hope.

Tiger Lily didn't need to say much to her grandmother's horse. The mare moved, sure-footed and determined, as if she'd ridden this route every day of her life. The truth was, though she had spent many years resting back at the village, she had a good memory. Head and ears down, she was a comfort to Tiger Lily, who was so anxious that she might have forgotten how to inhale if not for the horse's loud reminder in her own steady breath.

Just breathe, the horse's steady footfalls reminded her.

Just breathe, her loud heartbeat commanded.

The sun was still hidden, and rain had begun to

fall, soft and uneven, like the sky was still deciding if it would bother with inclement weather at all. As they drew closer, the rain became more constant, so that Tiger Lily had to squint against it. It painted the landscape a muted matte gray, making everything look too far away. She wondered if she should call out, start screaming. Maybe it would send a warning. Or maybe it would even scare off an attack. But before she could begin, they were at the hollow, galloping toward the little purse in the big tree.

"Sashi," she called out, dismounting before the horse had come to a complete stop. Newly made mud splashed up her pant legs as she ran to the tree. "Sashi, are you there?"

She finally released her held breath when the bag began to shimmy.

"Oh, thank goodness!" She even laughed a bit in her relief, imagining the state her friend must be in, being shouted awake. "Oh, Sashi, I'm sorry, but I—"

Just then the top of the purse opened, and out flew a large moth, beating its wings wildly in the rain, then grabbing the trunk to crawl up into dryer, quieter branches.

"Sashi?" Tiger Lily opened the purse wide and

peered inside. The little coin table was tipped on its side. From the pocket that had been made into a bed, an embroidered handkerchief was yanked so that it draped over the side. A small picture, framed with twine-wrapped sticks, had fallen from where it had been pinned to the fabric wall, and was busted on the floor. Tiger Lily knew one moth couldn't have done this much damage. No, something was wrong. Something had happened. And terrifyingly, she knew what it was.

"No! No! No!" She looked at the ground. The rain was making a mess out of the dirt, soggy and soaked. It beaded on the plants, formed rivulets in the grass, and was filling not only her own footprints, but two larger sets.

She was too late. They had already come and gone, and it was starting to look like they had taken Sashi with them.

Chapter Twelve

Sometimes when Tiger Lily felt really bad or really confused, that feeling settled into her bones, making it hard to move, so she could do nothing other than sit. It wasn't that she was tired or even directionless; it was like her body no longer knew how to work. That was exactly how Tiger Lily felt after the moth flew out of Sashi's house like a pale green siren and she understood that her friend had been grabbed up by pirates.

She would have sat right there, at the base of the tree, in the mud, but her grandmother's mare quietly walked over and nudged the girl's hands, which were holding each other, looking for comfort. The horse wouldn't let her sit, wouldn't let her fall into despair.

"Okay, okay . . ." Tiger Lily tried to push her away, but she wouldn't go. Finally, Tiger Lily grabbed a hold of the animal and swung herself up. She wasn't doing that consciously; it was an automatic motion—climbing on a horse's back. She could have done it in her sleep.

The horse walked slowly with the stunned girl on her back to a large pine tree and stood underneath. The thick branches were a perfect shelter from the rain, which was now coming down so hard it was the only sound in the world. Even then Tiger Lily didn't hear it. She kept seeing the empty purse and reviewing over and over in her mind the last conversation she'd overheard between Jukes and Jolly.

"Maybe we need to find our mast man."

"Ah! So we grab one of those kids up, then?"

"Looks like, Jolly, looks like."

Tiger Lily was disappointed in herself; why hadn't she put together that they'd meant the fairies? Surely she should have considered it? And Sashi lived on her own, making her an easy target. Not to mention the fact that she liked to go down to the beach to look for trinkets for her jewelery—the same beach where the pirates would have come ashore.

The issue was she had underestimated the pirates, the brute Bill Jukes and even the less menacing Jolly. They were dangerous, and sometimes dangerous people could have moments of devious brilliance. Not that it would have taken a flash of brilliance to put this one together.

"I really should have figured it out," she said out loud.

She was glad it was raining—if she could even feel such a thing as gladness. It was what she deserved—to be wet and uncomfortable and sad. After all, she had known the pirates were skulking around Neverland, and she hadn't done anything about it besides observe them in secret. Why had she thought she could handle this on her own? Why had she waited so long before attempting to tell her grandmother or one of the hunters? Was she so proud that she had made such a misstep?

The mare nickered underneath her, and Tiger Lily snapped out of it. There was no time to feel sorry for herself—not when Sashi needed her, not when there was no one else she could turn to. She could hear her grandmother's voice in her head: *Feeling sorry for yourself is not action; it's about as still as you can get. So when things need fixing, feeling sorry for yourself is the last thing you should be doing.*

She needed to move—and now. Sashi might not be that far away.

She clicked her tongue and set the horse moving. They had just gotten past Sashi's clearing when the rain stopped, all at once, and suddenly it felt like even the sky was on her side. She picked up the track of the two kidnappers from their footprints, not to mention the broken mess of branches and plants they had left in their clumsy wake, and followed at a brisk pace, checking now and then to make sure she was still going the right way.

She followed the tracks all the way to the beach, where their steps got steadier and approached the water's edge.

"Oh, no, no, no . . ." Tiger Lily knew if they'd made it to a boat, the trail would go cold. She wouldn't be able to follow, not now and not on horseback.

Her heart sank when the steps disappeared at the wet shore. A deep groove from the bottom of a small heavy boat was still indented in the silt.

"No!"

But then she caught movement out on the water,

and hope jumped into her throat. There, about a half mile out, was a boat, and inside the boat were two men—one rowing, one sitting straight and tall in the bow.

"There you are!"

She watched them, not caring if they saw her on the shore. She was already thinking about how she would board Hook's ship, how she could manage to grab back her friend from a vessel crawling with the worst pirates Neverland had ever known, when the little boat did something curious.

Instead of heading straight toward Skull Rock, where the *Jolly Roger* was docked, they turned sharply and headed west.

"Where are you going?" She chewed her lip, watching their progress. She didn't like that they were acting out of character. She'd learned that an animal that acted out of character was an animal you should avoid, like the bear. It was fear and confusion that had made it attack the people. Things like sickness or fear or greed made an animal act that way, and you did not want any part of it. It was impossible to know how to prepare when the next movements were not predictable. She thought the same must be true of pirates.

"What are you up to now?"

They were rowing back toward the shoreline near the old forest. It was a far side of the island she hardly ever went to. She watched for another few minutes, until she saw that there was no further trickery, that they hadn't spotted her and taken a different route; then she coaxed the mare west.

"Keep your eyes open," she told her. "We have to find Sashi and avoid the thieves who grabbed her, all at the same time."

If they were going to the Hilly Woods, she would find them. And if they indeed had her best friend, she was going to get her back.

Chapter Thirteen

When she had been little, littler than she was now, Tiger Lily had wished to be big enough to ride horses all afternoon, to be more of a helper to her beloved grandmother, to be able to venture out on her own with her friends. Her grandmother had sat her down, night after night, asking her questions about this desire.

"Do you really want to grow up?"

"Oh, yes. I want to be tall enough to pick apples and strong enough to hunt," she said, adamant. Being a small child was wearing thin. All she heard, among the lovely things she had grown used to, were all the nos and all the can'ts.

No, you can't go out, it's getting dark.

No, you can't come with us, you might get hurt.

"What is it that you want, exactly?" her grandmother asked, leaning in close, so Tiger Lily knew she was serious. She didn't get louder when she wanted people to pay attention; she got quieter so she could be sure you were listening. "And be specific."

Tiger Lily spoke for a long time. She wanted strong legs that could run for miles without cramping. She wanted to carry when they harvested so that her grandmother wouldn't have to do as much. She wanted to swim in the water without someone watching from the shore. She wanted freedom.

"But, my girl, the age you speak of is not all freedom. With age comes responsibility. You can do more, so you should do more." She chuckled. "It's not all horse riding and adventure."

Tiger Lily had closed her lips tight and thought for a minute. Then she nodded once and declared, "It's worth it."

The Elder laughed when she said it, so sure of herself.

"I can see by the look on your face that you are ready. Already stubborn and full of confidence. That's a good sign, for sure."

Back then, Tiger Lily's parents explained the process to her: she would go to sleep, and if she had the right dream and the right heart, she would wake up older. So she had concentrated as she drifted off, on being a bigger, stronger person, and when she woke up, her bed seemed a little bit smaller. She had done it! There was a celebration that day, and everyone brought her gifts, including the new clothes she would need for her new size.

The next few days she moved like a baby deer, all wobbly and tipping over. She couldn't figure out her joints, didn't know how to carry her new weight. She spent hours at the freshwater stream staring at her changed reflection.

"Wow, you're starting to act like a mermaid," Sashi had joked. "Let's just go already! We have so much to do."

And they did. Tiger Lily was now a tall girl who looked to be in the last years of childhood. Her shoulders were broader, and her hair was longer, and she could reach apples and pull them down without real effort. The best part was she fit on Pony better, like a real rider should.

And oh, was Pony surprised to see her with her new aged body. The first day she went to the horse meadow, her grandmother warned her to take things slow, told her Pony might take some time to get used to this new version of her. And boy, did he jump when she called for him. She didn't want to be mean, but his little jump, which made him drop a mouthful of grass and stumble a bit to the side, made her laugh. And it was a good thing, because her laugh reassured him: this tall, beautiful girl was still, in fact, his sweet little Tiger Lily. It was a short adjustment period after that, both horse and rider learning how to coordinate their bodies so that they could run together.

She thought about those days now, riding a different horse into a darkened patch of woods.

As they galloped over the distance between the beach and the Hilly Woods, she kept thinking: *What if I hadn't lied to Sashi about following the pirates? What if I'd invited her to come with me, and she'd heard them, too? Maybe she would have been prepared. Maybe she would have stayed in the community with me instead of all alone in her purse. Maybe she would have avoided the beach, where she could be easily spotted.*

"Good job," she told herself. "You wanted to protect the ones you love by going all rogue and doing this alone, and you ended up hurting exactly the one you love."

The forest wasn't exactly scary, not any more than any other forest could be—dark in places, shadows under every tree. But now it was absolutely terrifying, full of danger and what-ifs. What if she didn't get there in time? What if they hurt her friend? She felt certain that Sashi didn't know any more about the Andon than she did. What if they decided the fairy was lying and holding out on them?

"Okay, girl, I've got things from here," she whispered, patting the mare along her mane. "You stay. I don't need any more friends pulled into all this."

She bent her knee to swing her leg over in a smooth dismount, but the mare neighed and walked into the trees.

"Whoa, whoa, girl," Tiger Lily commanded. "Stop! I'm getting off now. You wait here."

But the horse didn't stop. She stepped carefully over roots that had erupted from the loam, and turned her large body in gentle curves to avoid fallen branches and rotting logs.

After a few more tries, Tiger Lily stopped fussing.

"Okay, then, you win. Maybe it's time I had a partner, anyway."

Here the ground was covered in mushrooms: puffballs so big it looked like the trees were blowing bubbles, lion's manes so full they looked like little people with long hair, and ladders of Chaga climbing the bark like soft steps. Pointy white trillium flowers lay open like tired children splayed in the half-light. And from everywhere came the sounds of the creatures who called this magical place home. Tiger Lily picked up the calls of chirping insects, the whistles of curious birds, and the skittering of small paws from every direction. On a different day, it would have been enchanting. But that day, as she searched for her friend, everything was a potential threat, like the sound of pirates closing in.

"Easy now, easy," she whispered to the horse, who seemed to be handling this much better than she was. "Steady, girl. We'll be okay."

She was obviously trying to reassure herself.

Suddenly, there was the sound of breathing, quick and full. Both girl and horse stiffened and paused, their own breaths held, to listen.

From the left came movement, and a young deer stepped near them from a small circle of birch trees.

He saw them right away, lifted his neck straight, and, ready to bolt, looked between the horse and her rider.

The mare lifted her front leg and put it down gently, as if tapping the ground—twice. She lowered her head and then raised it, slowly. The deer watched. And after a moment, he too tapped the forest floor, twice. Tiger Lily was still holding her breath when he turned and walked back the way he had come. He looked once over his shoulder, and then the mare began to follow.

Tiger Lily emptied her lungs finally. Were they following the deer? And even more amazing, was this deer leading them?

They climbed up a slight embankment, stepped across a shallow stream fed by the big waters of the bay, and stopped just past the where the line of tall trees devolved into dense shrubs. Beyond the shrubs lay a rocky beach, and on the beach was a heavy wooden boat with two dirty men dragging it up onto land.

Bill Jukes and Jolly!

With a look around, Jukes reached into the boat and pulled out a large glass jar with a silver screw-top lid. And inside the jar was her very angry, very scared friend Sashi. The pirate put his massive face to the side of the jar and laughed, showing all his sharp teeth.

Chapter Fourteen

It took everything in her not to storm onto the beach and trample the men under the weight of her grandmother's horse. But she knew that rushing out there could put Sashi in danger; she'd either be knocked about in the fray by accident or harmed by one of the pirates on purpose. So Tiger Lily stayed where they had stopped, just out of sight, so close and yet so far away, to come up with a plan.

The mare gave a soft nicker, like a whisper, and bowed slightly. Just then, the deer turned and dashed back into the thick of the woods. Tiger Lily nodded in his direction, a silent thanks for his help.

A voice boomed out from the shoreline: it belonged to Bill Jukes. "What's that?"

"Where?" Jolly answered.

"Over there," Jukes replied.

"Uhhhhh, a deer, I think," Jolly answered.

"Bah, you wouldn't know a deer from a deck cat, you."

"Maybe so, but that weren't no cat."

Tiger Lily held her breath. If they came near her now, she might get away, but they would know for sure that they were being followed. She waited.

"All right, then, let's get a fire goin' and cook up these fish," Jukes said finally.

"I'm sick of fish," Jolly complained. "Why do we always gotta have fish?"

"Well, then, maybe you oughta go after your man the deer, then. Catch us some venison for dinner." Jukes's answer was dripping with sarcasm.

"I don't think pirates can hunt, Jukesy." Jolly's answer was quiet, maybe even a little embarrassed.

"Oh, then maybe that explains all the fish, don't it?"

Tiger Lily led the mare back into the trees and dismounted without a sound. Then she followed the shadows as they moved along the beach and stopped at an area that had already been set up as a camp of sorts. She settled in to watch, keeping a close eye on Sashi.

"Musta been others here," Jukes observed, touching a cutlass at his waist. "Hope they're long gone. If they come back, I'll give them a surprise, all right."

"Yeah! This is our spot now!" Jolly yelled out, braver. He hung the handle of the jar on a low branch, jostling Sashi to and fro.

"And don't you worry, my little friend." Jukes tapped the glass separating Sashi from the sky. "We'll get to you soon enough."

"You think she'll talk?" Jolly was already skewering a few skinny fish with a stick.

"She ain't got a choice now, does she? Good thing I spent all that time learnin' their silly bell language, eh?" Jukes laughed, turning to his friend. He sighed. "Well, now, why ya sticking the fish? Ya gotta make the fire first!"

By the time they got the fire going and began an argument about who was going to get the bigger fish and why, Tiger Lily knew she was in for a wait. After they ate, she watched them play a game of dice, burping their dinner and rubbing their bellies. She listened as they made a plan to sleep before interrogating their prisoner. After all, it was already late.

"Sure is," she whispered to herself, stifling a yawn. If they were going to sleep, that meant she had a chance to sneak in later and snatch Sashi. All she had to do was wait. She made her way silently back to her horse and got comfortable. It was going to be a long night.

Tiger Lily waited so long she fell asleep. The shush of the waves and the slow serenade of crickets in concert made it impossible to stay awake. Plus, the moss was cool and the ground was damp, so she had to curl up, pushing aside her mare, who was already breathing the deep breaths of slumber.

She woke up suddenly.

The mare was snuffling her ribs. Tiger Lily sat up with a start, confused at first by the open sky and the horse in her bed. And then she remembered: she wasn't in her bed. She was out in the Hilly Woods, where it changed into the far shore on the Neversea, and she was here to help get Sashi back from the pirates.

"Oh, I hope I didn't make noise in my sleep," she whispered to the horse, rubbing her muzzle.

"Enough to wake us up, missus," someone replied.

Tiger Lily jumped, spun, and stood in one quick movement. Behind her were a yawning Jolly and a smiling Bill Jukes, and in his hand was Sashi in her jar, with a look of fear and disappointment stamped on her little face.

"Oh, Sashi. I'm sorry." Tiger Lily barely had time to get the words out before the pirates were on her.

Chapter Fifteen

The sun came up like every morning, oblivious to the fact that things were very, very wrong. It rose above Skull Rock, where the *Jolly Roger* would be docked. It filled the empty fields and walkways of the village. It tried to pry its rays into the Lost Boys' house, but they had the windows locked against it with bedsheets and boards. It even ran its warm fingers over the circle of birch where a small camp was built around a smoking firepit, where two pirates snored, a fairy banged her fists against a glass jar, and Tiger Lily lay tied to the trunk of a tree.

"Sashi . . . cut it out. You're just gonna hurt yourself." Tiger Lily was exhausted both from trying to escape for the past few hours and the defeat that had settled into her bones. She wasn't even sure her friend could hear her. The jar she was imprisoned in had been hung from a branch across the clearing from where Tiger Lily was tied with salt water–logged ropes, the smell of fish filling her nostrils.

Finally, Bill Jukes roused from his loud sleep, stretching big and lazily as he stood. He yawned so hugely the black teeth at the back of his jaw were exposed. He scratched his belly and looked around, finally seeing his newest prisoner, who was watching him with wary eyes.

"Ah! G'morning, then. And how'd you sleep at Camp Jukes?" He bowed low, mocking her grimace both at his disheveled appearance and at the impossible predicament she found herself in. "Got any complaints, missus?"

He pulled her sheath out of his jacket pocket, yanked her blade free, and held it up in the sun. "Didn't get a good look at this when we took it offa ya last night." He ran a thumb across the sharp edge, and a line of red blood popped up from the sliced skin. "Sharp, that! I think I'll keep this. As a souvenir."

Laughing, he put it back in his pocket, then wandered off into the bushes, stopping on his way to kick his partner awake. "Oi! Get up, you great hog. I'm going to see to my morning relief. You keep an eye on the ladies, eh?"

Jolly didn't even cry out. Tiger Lily got the sense that being kicked awake wasn't unusual for him. "All right, I got 'em."

Despite his reply, Jolly went right back to sleep, his gravelly snores pouring into the trees like predators' growls.

"I mean it," Jukes, just out of sight, shouted from a nearby bush. "Get up or I'll wear your skin!" He was terrifying when he was angry.

Jolly snorted himself awake and sat up, his eyes still closed and his mouth hanging open. "I'm up!"

The men bumbled about, trying to restart the fire, scrounging for wood, then arguing over some hard bread they split between them from one of their packsacks.

"Shouldn't we feed them?" Jolly asked, looking almost shyly at their forced guests.

"Well"—Jukes considered, chewing loudly with his

bad teeth—"if you is such a humanitarian, their take comes from yours. Ain't hardly enough here for me." He indicated his own hunk of bread, then patted his stomach. "I'm still a growing boy."

Jolly tried to curve his shoulders in so that he wouldn't have to look at the girls and ate greedily. But eventually, he sighed, stood, and split the remainder of his piece. He unscrewed the cap of the jar, and for a moment, Tiger Lily had a glimmer of hope.

"Go, go!" She screamed it so suddenly that the men were distracted, both looking at her. Sashi pushed off the bottom curve of the jar and headed for the opening.

"Jolly, the fairy!" Jukes yelled.

He clamped his meaty palm over the opening, and the top of Sashi's head collided with his flesh. She fell back to the bottom like a swatted fly.

"Sashi!" Tiger Lily yelled, seeing her friend lying still. "Sashi, are you hurt?"

Jukes was on his feet. Glaring at Jolly, he grabbed the metal lid from him and took the jar.

Jolly looked hurt. "What? Don't get all sore at me. I was just tryna be a gentleman like."

The taller man closed one eye and peered into the jar. He shook the container a bit, then said, "She's all right. Knocked out, I s'pose, but that's her own fault, and yours." He looked pointedly across the clearing at Tiger Lily. "Giving bad advice."

With the top firmly screwed on and the jar hung back in the tree, the men finished their breakfast and then talked in low whispers to each other. Tiger Lily wouldn't have been able to make out their words even if she had been trying, and at that moment, she was concentrating on the jar, watching her friend, who was still sprawled out along the bottom of the glass.

"All right, then, here's how it's gonna be," Jukes said loudly. He paced in front of Tiger Lily, his hands on his hips, kicking his feet out as he stepped, keeping his back very straight. She supposed he was trying to look serious. "When your little friend there wakes up, we're gonna have a chat, see. And one of yous is gonna tell us all about the treasure."

He gave her his best scary face, narrowing one eye and clenching his teeth.

"Are you sick?" she asked gently.

He was startled. He looked back at Jolly, who shrugged, and then down at the girl. "No. Why?"

"Well, you just suddenly looked like you might have

to throw up," she said, teasing him and keeping a straight face. "That is not a very scary look, friend."

"Well, well," he scoffed. He acted as if her jab meant nothing, but his cheeks reddened. "We'll see who's full of jokes and vinegar when I'm pulling the wings off a fairy, then, eh?"

That remark suddenly made Tiger Lily feel like she might be the one to throw up. He really could do whatever he wanted, and there wasn't anything she could do to stop him. How could she keep Sashi safe? She couldn't even get her hands free to save herself. Then she had an idea.

She looked the man dead in the eye. "There's no need. I'll tell you where it is."

"What? Just like that? *Pfft.*" He laughed. "I bet shingles to shinies you haven't the foggiest where the treasure even is. Probably don't even know what we're talking about. No, it's the fairy who'll—"

"The Andon, right?" She interrupted him. "That's what you're looking for?"

He stopped pacing. In fact, it sounded like he'd stopped breathing. He turned and quickly glanced at his partner, whose eyes had gotten big. He bent down so that he was suddenly right in Tiger Lily's face. She could smell his black teeth. She turned her face to the side so she could breathe a little better.

"Where'd you hear about the Andon, then?"

Tiger Lily took a deep breath and turned back to the man, smiling secretively, trying to match her voice to that fake smile, trying to sound sure of herself and not as scared as she actually was.

"Oh, I know things. In fact, I know everything there is to know about Neverland." She held up her chin, hoping she looked smug—defiant, even. "You might say I know more than anyone else who has ever called this place home."

Jukes rubbed his chin with his dirty fingers. "Is that really and truly so?"

"It is," she replied. "Really and truly."

Thinking, Jukes walked to the firepit and kicked at the wood, which they had still not gotten aflame, sending the logs flying. "Well, then, I suppose we don't need the fairy."

By then, Sashi had roused. She was sitting on her bottom, rubbing her head, her curls sticking out, all wild and tangled.

"That is right." Tiger Lily was hopeful. *Yes, this could work!* "So you can just let her go."

She saw Jukes's shoulders rise and fall with laughter. Her hope faded away, but she kept the smile on her face all the same.

"Let her go, eh?" Jukes clasped his hands behind his wide back and walked toward Sashi's jar.

"Yes. I mean, why bother keeping her locked up? Just seems like more of a bother than it's worth." Tiger Lily tried to shrug, but the ropes made movement difficult. "Just let the little thing go. What threat could she possibly be to two strong seafarers such as yourselves?"

Jukes looked at her between the strands of dirty blond hair that hung down his forehead. It was a quizzical look, as if he were trying to solve a numbers problem. Uh-oh, maybe she was laying it on a little thick.

Jolly cleared his throat and tossed his filthy ponytail over his shoulder. "She ain't wrong. We is pretty strong, after all, and the fairy is just a bitty thing."

"Yes," Jukes hissed. "Yes, I suppose that's true. But you know what? I think maybe we'll hold on to the little sprite."

Calm down, Tiger Lily, she thought. *Don't mess this up now.* "What's the point?" she asked out loud.

"Point is . . ." Jukes said, tapping a dirty fingernail

against the glass jar. Sashi stuck out her tongue at him. "This little sprite, why, she is tiny, but you know what she does have? A big mouth. She could go runnin' all sorts a' places and go yapping about."

"She wouldn't. Sashi isn't like that!" Tiger Lily said. Her voice cracked and wavered.

"Ah, so Sashi, is it? You two know each other, then?"

He smiled sinisterly. Now he knew Tiger Lily cared. That meant he knew she was probably lying and would say anything to save her friend. She tried to cover her mistake by acting nonchalant, even though her heart hammered away.

"I know of her," she said. "Neverland is not a big place, after all. And I'm just saying she is not the kind of fairy who would go around telling other people's business."

Jukes walked away from the jar and back toward Tiger Lily, then bent his considerable size and crouched down right in front of her. He cocked his head to the side and waited until she made eye contact; then he leaned in and began talking to her slowly, as if she were a little child with no sense.

"Here's what I think. I think you two is close.

Close enough for you to come out here all willy-nilly to save her. Now, Jolly and I have gotten pretty busted up out there searching for this here Andon, and we is tired. . . ."

"So tired," Jolly agreed.

"So you're gonna go get the thing for us. And us? Well, we is gonna wait right here for you to deliver it to us." He looked back at his mate. "Sound good, Jolly? Fancy a little break, eh?"

"Yeah, Jukes. Sounds right good." He was already lying on his back, his arms crossed under his head, as if he were starting a little vacation at the beach. "Get some sun on the old cheeks."

Tiger Lily narrowed her eyes. She was so mad she wanted to scream. But now wasn't the time for reacting to others' bad behavior. She had to keep a level head. "And why would I do anything for you? You haven't promised me anything in return."

"Because, my dear, should you decide to run off or to gather up some folks to come back, well, I'll take that jar with your little friend inside and I'll toss it in the Neversea. And as I've been kind enough to poke some breathin' holes in the top, I'm guessing it won't take long for the water to rush right in and down through those holes, and then . . ." He shrugged dramatically. "Well, then we'll see how long a jar with a fairy can actually float."

He watched her, and when her reaction to the image of her friend tumbling in slow motion to the bottom of the sea flashed across her face, he pantomimed crying, mocking her real terror. And then he laughed. Soon Jolly joined in and they were cackling like old hags.

If Tiger Lily could have gotten free of her restraints then, she would have fought them both, and she was so angry she was sure she would have won. But the ropes around her held fast, and all she could envision was a little glass jar sinking into the depths of the Neversea waves.

She took a deep breath. "If you promise to release her when I get back . . . I'll do it."

Chapter
Sixteen

S he had very little time to find and bring the Andon to the pirates. They said she had till the sun switched places with the moon, and then till the new sun sat just above Skull Rock like a crown, or Sashi would be fish food. Tiger Lily's community wouldn't be back from fishing for days, and riding out to find them was pointless when they could have been anywhere, following the school of fish wherever it decided to lead them. No, she was on her own this time.

When they released her from her ropes, she sprang up and moved quickly just out of reach of their long arms and dirty hands. Then she yelled to Sashi, "I'll be back. I am going to save you!"

Her friend beat her wings inside her prison in response. Tiger Lily sighed. She couldn't even hear the bells sewn on Sashi's dress. They always sounded a merry song when she fluttered her wings against the sky. Tiger Lily would have done anything to hear them again, to see Sashi free above her head, where she belonged. Sashi blew her a kiss, and Tiger Lily blew one back at her.

"Ah, ain't that sweet," Jukes teased, blowing exaggerated kisses to Jolly, who giggled in return and pretended to be bashful.

Tiger Lily pointed a finger at them. "You hurt her before I get back and you'll have the entire island to answer to," she yelled, her hands balled up into fists.

She turned and ran off into the forest before either of the pirates could answer.

Her grandmother's horse was waiting for her, right where Tiger Lily had left her at the edge of the woods. Grasping the reigns, she used a rock to jump up and land directly on the mare's back.

"Go!"

And then they were off, galloping dangerously fast for such a narrow, twisty path. She couldn't slow down—not now. She certainly couldn't stop. At that moment she thought of being forced to move against her will, to run until there was no breath left in her body. That was what this felt like. A life depended on her.

While the mare navigated the forest, Tiger Lily racked her brain. Where could she go? She didn't know anything about the Andon, and she had only a night to figure it out and then get the thing.

They finally burst out of the trees and picked up even more speed crossing the field. Tiger Lily realized she hadn't given any direction to the horse. After considering for a moment, she leaned down close to the mare's ear. "We need to get to the Lost Boys."

The answer from the horse was to take a sharp turn to the left, and then they were headed full tilt for Fort Fierce. She knew the Lost Boys didn't have any answers, but at the very least, maybe they could lend her a bow. She didn't even have her trusty knife anymore. It hurt to think of her precious tool—gifted to her by her favorite auntie—being held by one of the kidnappers.

"Probably not even holding it right," she muttered.

She started calling for them before she even got to the fort.

"Lost Boys? Wake up. It's an emergency!" She shouted through her cupped hands to make her voice as loud as it could be so that even if they weren't in the fort, if they had fallen asleep in the woods, as they did from time to time, they would hear her. "Nibs, Curly, twins . . . get up! I need you!"

The thing with the Lost Boys was this: they might have been mischievous, and they were definitely messy, but when push came to shove, if you were their friend, they would have your back. They were loyal and brave and ready for a tussle. And that was exactly the kind of friends she needed right then.

She dismounted while the horse was still moving and scaled the tree to the fort lickety-split. She burst through the opening in the floor like a thrown rock, all speed and momentum. On the ground were little piles of nut shells, with many more scattered around, like they'd had a feast and then used the leavings to wage war on one another. But there were no children here.

"Oh, come on," she huffed. "Where are you now?"

She went to the crude window and scanned the

ground below. Then she cupped her hands again and called out.

"Lost Boys, it's Tiger Lily. I need you! Now!"

There was sudden movement in the trees and then the sound of squirrels fighting, and then four bodies rushed into the clearing, each one in a different state of sleepiness. Nibs didn't even have his eyes open yet, but he was already feeling around on the ground for rocks to put into his slingshot. Turning this way and that to cover the area, Curly had an arrow nocked, her bow flexed to a smooth curve. The twins were running in all directions at once. This was their own specialty: scouting as fast as possible and causing confusion. Judging by their plentiful supply of food and furs, it must have been surprisingly effective on their hunting expeditions.

"Oi, TL!" Curly shouted. They didn't know where she was, only that she needed them.

Tiger Lily put her fingers in her mouth the way Sashi had taught her and let out a shrill whistle. "Up here!"

Four sets of eyes lifted to the sky and found her hanging out the side of the tree house, waving. "I'm coming down."

Tiger Lily didn't bother with the steps on the trunk. Instead, she balanced on the window's edge and jumped, then landed in a somersault and flipped back onto her feet. "Okay, listen. . . ."

She took a beat to catch her breath, then continued, "Sashi has been captured by the pirates."

"The stinky pirates!" The twins screamed it out and ran off in opposite directions, then doubled back only to slam into each other and land flat on their bottoms.

Nibs began to laugh before he took in what Tiger Lily had said. "Wait, what do you mean 'captured'?"

"I mean they grabbed Sashi from her bed, threw her in a jar, and took her to the beach by the Hilly Woods," Tiger Lily said quickly. She could barely breathe. She felt like she had been running instead of her horse.

"Okay, okay." Curly approached her slowly. "Relax, Lily. Just breathe for a moment. Nibs," she called over her shoulder. "Help the twins up and get them right. Sounds like we have work to do."

It wasn't more than five minutes later that the children, all the sleep knocked out of their heads, had gathered in a small circle and were listening to Tiger Lily recount her tale.

"I'll find 'em!" Nibs shouted, standing up in anger

and kicking rocks into the bushes. "I'll tie *them* to a tree and see how they like it. And then I'll—"

"Easy now, tiger," Curly said softly. "Let's gather our weapons. Twin One, get the slingshots and jam as many rocks as you can into your pockets."

The girl saluted and ran off.

"Two, you fetch my arrows. They're hidden in the old oak by the frog hole. Grab them all."

"On it!"

"Nibs? Nibs, you listening, man?"

It took a moment, but eventually Nibs stopped punching the air in a pretend fight with imaginary pirates and came back to the circle.

"You need to dig up those sharp sticks from where we put 'em to hide them from the twins so they wouldn't poke each other's eyes out. We'll need them now."

Curly sighed, running her hands through her tangled hair. Tiger Lily watched her with admiration in her eyes. She hadn't needed to correct Curly or give orders. Instead, she had allowed Curly to lead. But she also knew she needed to continue to be a leader herself. Soon she was examining their meager weapons and realizing, unhappily, that they were unfit for battle.

"I just don't know how we do this without Sashi

getting hurt," Tiger Lily said with a sigh. "None of us have been in a proper fight before with another person, let alone with two grown pirates."

"Pirates are nothing but smelly scoundrels," Curly spat. "We can take 'em."

"But we'll have to guarantee that Sashi will be safe. All they have to do is toss her in the sea, and that's not hard to do; it won't take but a second, just one second when we're not winning, and it's all over. We can't let them run off with her. If they get to their boat, we'll need a plan for how to catch them."

Curly stood, listening, with her hands on her hips. "What do you think we need, Lily? Is there something or someone that could help? Someone who's fought pirates before?"

Tiger Lily considered this. There weren't many people who had willingly crossed paths with the *Jolly Roger* crew in recent times. "When's Peter coming back?"

Curly shook her head. "Hasn't been seen since the day after the bear, and we don't know when he'll be back. He left with Tink."

"Hmmm." She wished she were in her caves. That was the one place where it was easy to clear her mind when she needed to think about serious things. She could see the old painting there now if she closed her eyes. "If only Grandma hadn't gone on the fishing trip. She would know what to do."

"That's exactly who we need!" Curly cried out, excited. "Let's go get her. What are you hanging around with us poor saps for? You are related to an honest-to-goodness hero!"

"Because she's not home. No one is. They're out fishing, and that could mean they're anywhere by now—just depends on where the fish decided to lead them. I have no idea how fish think." She sighed again. "Otherwise, I would have gone there first, not here. If only there was a way to find them . . ."

Curly looked a bit hurt by that, even though she must know it was the truth. Tiger Lily kicked an apple that lay on the ground, and, having returned, Nibs chased after it, then shined it on the front of his black shirt before biting into it.

"Seems to me," he said with a full mouth, "you either need the grandma or you need the Andon, maybe both."

Tiger Lily let out a frustrated yell. "*Argh!* Both are impossible. Is there even a treasure to be gotten? If you don't know about the Andon, and the nosy mermaids don't know about the Andon, who would know?"

The Lost Boys looked at one another but didn't say a word.

Tiger Lily caught their exchange of glances. "What? What is it?"

"Well . . ." Curly stalled. "It's probably nothing."

"What's probably nothing?" Tiger Lily grabbed her by the shoulders. "I'm desperate here! What is it?"

"Just tell her about the old lady, then," Twin Two said. She had lain down on her back in a patch of dirt and was kicking her legs in and out and waving her arms above her head to make a "filth fairy" in the sand and dust. She'd grown bored, since it had become clear they were not marching off into battle anytime soon.

Curly sighed. "There is a witch. . . ."

"A witch?" Tiger Lily repeated it as a question. "Like a real witch, here in Neverland?"

"Yes, a witch. And she's here but also not here."

Tiger Lily groaned. "I swear, if one more person feeds me riddles . . ."

"No, listen. I mean she's here, but you can't just get to her any normal way. You have to sort of wish for her. She decided a long time ago to live alone, when the pirates came and people started fighting. She hates fighting."

She was nervous. Tiger Lily was clearly not in the mood for stories.

"And you gotta bring a present," Two called from her cloud of dirt. "She's like a kid. We all like presents. It's the way to our heart."

"She likes books best," Nibs remarked as he chewed. "Best to bring a book."

"And she knows about the Andon?" Tiger Lily couldn't be bothered to question the likelihood of this tale. She was willing to try just about anything at this point.

"She knows about everything, they say," Curly replied, nodding. "So, yes, if there is an Andon, she'd be your best chance to hear about it."

"Maybe she has a map," Nibs shouted. "I love a good map, I do."

Tiger Lily squared her shoulders and lifted her chin, trying to look brave so maybe she would feel brave. "All right, I'm game. Let's call the witch."

"Okay, then. But you gotta wait for the moon to come out. That's when you do it," Curly informed her.

"But that's not for ages! That means once we know

about the treasure, and maybe where it is, we'll only have till the sun reaches Skull Rock to go get it and bring it to the shore. And even then, how do we make sure we're not double-crossed? They have weapons, Curly. Real weapons, not just sticks and rocks." She thought hard. What did she need to do right then? It was usually her grandmother who stepped in to help her puzzle through her problems. "I know my village could help. There must be a way to find them. Let's think."

Curly rubbed her jaw and thought. "I wish we had a bird's-eye view."

"Of the island? Me too." Tiger Lily thought. Though she'd told the pirates that Neverland wasn't very big, she knew it was bigger than it seemed. She used to think it would seem smaller, more knowable, the taller she got, but the opposite was true. "Wait, a bird's-eye view?"

"That's what I said," Curly responded.

An idea started to form in Tiger Lily's mind. "Grandma always takes care of the birds. And when someone does you a favor, you want to return it, don't you?"

She was asking Curly, but really she was just thinking out loud. Nevertheless, the child nodded in response.

Tiger Lily smiled. "Curly, can you call those birds you've been training?"

Catching on, Curly smiled, then lifted her chin and called out to the sky.

Chapter
Seventeen

First the sky was dotted with dark bodies that circled above. Then they began to caw, calling out to others. And soon the air was filled with so many birds they were like a dark cloud, raining down into the field. Tiger Lily waited for the crows to stop chatting among themselves, but when it was apparent they would not stop on their own, she cleared her throat and spoke out loudly.

"Ah, good morning, folks. Thank you for coming." She wasn't sure how to proceed. How did one give a speech to a field full of loud, crabby birds? She looked at the Lost Boys, who shrugged in response.

"So, I have asked you—or rather my friend Curly here asked you—all here to make a request."

Immediately they started chattering again, squawking and shrieking to one another. They clearly weren't impressed. They had been summoned to do work for a near stranger, and a flightless one at that? They didn't like doing things for the ones they did know.

"I know, I know," she said, raising her voice. "But I specifically asked for the crows because I need the bravest of the birds today."

One by one, the crows began to quiet down. Yes, they agreed with this flightless girl: they were the bravest.

"And the strongest!"

More of the chatterboxes closed their beaks and turned one eye or the other toward her, not being able to look straight ahead, since their eyes were on the sides of their heads.

"I need the ones who understand the importance of friendship, who are known for being the most loyal friend a creature could have."

Soon there was complete silence, with every bird paying attention. It was a bit intimidating. Tiger Lily looked at the Lost Boys again, who again all responded with the same motion, each giving her two thumbs up.

She rolled her eyes at them. Fat lot of help they were being.

"A friend of mine—my best friend, in fact—has been captured by pirates." There was one lone squawk from the bunch. She nodded toward the voice. "Yes, yes, thank you. I agree, it is terrible. And I need to get her back. But for this, I need my community. And that's where you come in."

She was pacing now, in front of a hundred black crows, who turned their heads to follow her movement. It was like she had her own tiny army at her command.

"I will need the bravest, the fastest, the best of the crows to fly out over Neverland and find my family. They are on a fishing trip and could be anywhere by now. These birds will have to locate them and then get them to return to help."

At this, the talk erupted again. She could guess what they were conversing about. "I know, I understand. You are worried because most humans don't even try to understand birds. They aren't as . . . smart as some of the other animals. But there is one among them who will try—my great-great-grandmother."

There was some low chattering between the biggest

of the crows, the ones who had lived the longest and seen the most. Several heads turned, and soon they were puffing out their chest feathers to show that they were brave and their opinions mattered.

"Yes, some of you know her. She leaves aside a portion of her garden's harvest every year for you and your families. She feeds you and will continue to feed you for as long as she has that garden, even when the harvest is lean, even when we are hungry, because it's the right thing to do. She always gives back. And now I am asking you if you will give back. I am asking if you will go and find her and bring her home. I need her help. Without it, well, I may never see my friend again."

Now that she had invoked the name of her matriarch, the crows were raring to go. They flew up, twisting into one huge, loud tornado of feather and sound, tunneling into the sky. Their wings beating all at once moved the grass and the trees and blew Tiger Lily's hair up and away from her head. Some of it even got snagged by claws and branches.

"Hurry," she yelled to them. "We don't have much time!"

When they reached the tops of the trees, they dispersed, like glass marbles bursting out of a split bag, pouring in all directions. Tiger Lily smiled. If anyone could find her people, it was these birds. She waved them off with both hands, then slapped her palms together, indicating a job well done.

"Well," she said, walking back to Curly and Nibs, the twins having run into the field to collect the thousands of loose feathers that were still falling into the grass like black snow, "I hope they can do it. No doubt they can, with all your careful training, Curly. Now, how do I find this witch who can direct me to the Andon, again?"

Curly smiled. "Well, for that, you'll need that book."

Then she turned on one heel and marched back to the fort. Tiger Lily ran to catch up to her.

"This is mine," Curly said, holding a book out to her. It was an old volume, the edges of the cover gnawed by mice, the pages wavy and yellow. "I've always had it. I think . . . maybe it belonged to someone I used to know. Perhaps my mother."

Tiger Lily had never held a book before. She hesitated, then took it in both hands. She knew how to read; her grandmother had made sure of that. But that was from single pages and letters drawn in the sand with a stick. And she had learned to write words in a few languages with paint on wood or stone or whatever was handy—syllabics and letters in blocky shapes and curvy lines. But she had never before held a real book. It was heavy. Understanding just how much was in a book, the weight made sense to her.

"Do you have a lot of things like this—from before?" She spoke kindly, with gentle tones. Everyone knew the Lost Boys yearned for a mother. They didn't know much about their families, and many had no memories at all, but each one of them was filled with an absence. That was probably what made them so messy and loud—trying to fill that hole.

"Nah." She turned away, not knowing what to do with her hands now that the book had left them. "Just that."

Tiger Lily reached out and grabbed the little girl's hand. "I can't take this. Not a book that means this much to you. But I am really grateful that you would even think to give it to me."

Curly squeezed her fingers and tried to smile. "It's yours now, Lil. I want you to have it."

"You gotta bring a gift to the witch," Nibs said, walking into the clearing. He had found another apple. "And you gotta think about her the whole walk. Like about finding her. That's how you get to her place."

Tiger Lily clasped the book to her chest. It smelled of old paper and new earth, which made sense, since it had been wrapped in a hide and buried for safekeeping.

"Oh, and you gotta follow the blue flowers." Nibs tossed the apple core and burped. "That's the path. Once you start to see them in a straight line, that's when you know you're on the way. It's a weird journey, but Peter says she's the one who knows everything. Besides him, o' course."

"Of course." Tiger Lily rolled her eyes. Peter Pan was her friend, and she loved him as such. But sometimes she didn't much like his bossy ways and oversized sense of importance.

Curly took a few steps back to the hole she had dug to get the book, and began kicking the loose dirt into place. "You go to the edge of our woods, stand where the moonlight is brightest, and concentrate."

Tiger Lily waited for her to continue, but she didn't say another word.

"And then what?" Tiger Lily asked.

"Then you wait."

She arched her eyebrows. "Wait for what, exactly?"

The children looked at each other. Neither of them had successfully found the witch before. Of course, neither had any reason to want to. It certainly wasn't worth giving up one of their treasures. And considering the witch loved books best and only Curly had a book, no one had a real chance of getting there.

"Well," Nibs said, "for the path, I suppose."

"So I'm supposed to stand in the moonlight, thinking about finding a witch I don't know, and then wait for blue flowers to grow?"

That couldn't be right. Flowers took weeks to properly grow.

"They's magic flowers, Lily," Twin One said as she and Twin Two wandered over. Her posture was stooped so that she looked like a little old woman, and her steps were measured and slow. Rocks bulged out from her pockets and made her clothes hang funny.

Twin One stopped in the midst of her friends and breathed heavily. "I don't know how much pirates I can chase," she huffed. "I'm feelin' a bit . . . tired all the sudden." Just then a rock fell out of her coat pocket and landed on her bare foot.

"Ow, ow, ow . . ." She jumped to lift weight off her hurt toes, and her balance tipped. She fell flat on her front, unable to turn, like an upended turtle, rocks tumbling every which way.

They couldn't help it: they all laughed. And soon so did the fallen girl, though her laughter was muffled in the ground. They flipped her over, emptied her pockets, and set her back on her feet. Curly checked out her foot to make sure she was okay.

"You'll live," she proclaimed, slapping the girl on her back. "You're a tough nut."

Curly turned to Tiger Lily and grew serious again. "So, you have to do this alone. That's how it's done."

"Sure. I can do that," she replied, staring at her own feet. "But how do you know that's how it's done? That this will even work?"

"Same way we know everything," Nibs said before biting into his next apple. "Stories."

"But we'll be close by, keeping an eye out," Curly said. "So you're safe."

"You'll take care of Grandma's horse till I get back?" she asked them.

"You know we will," Twin Two said.

"And one of you will go to the village to leave word

for them if they get back—where to find me and what's going on?"

"Already on the way," Nibs shouted, fitting his furry fox hood over his messy hair.

"Thank you." She smiled at each of them. "I mean it. Thank you so much."

They smiled back at her, then walked to the edge of the woods, where each Lost Boy would take a turn watching over their friend until the flowers bloomed and she was on her way.

Chapter Eighteen

S he closed her eyes now and then, squeezing them tight and thinking about what she needed the most: help. Each time she opened them, there was a little more green pushing up past the top of the grass, the beginnings of bella knots. These would become the path she had to follow.

Curly had fallen asleep on her shift and was snoring like a grown-up. Tiger Lily still stood in the same spot, holding the book to her chest, trying to focus on finding the witch who could help her hunt the Andon. She couldn't help giggling at the gravelly snores coming from the nearby cedars—and that was when the first flowers began to unfurl in the moonlight.

"Here we go," she whispered, and took the first step, putting her feet carefully between the bright blooms.

"Thank you," she whispered to the flowers that worked hard to grow fast so that she would find her way.

She followed the blue bella knots, each one the same shade, the same height and diameter, for what seemed like miles. Every now and again she would pause and look around, trying to keep track of where she was, but everything started to look different. Maybe it was that she didn't travel much at night. But maybe it was because she was headed into territory she had never been in before.

Hours passed. The path the flowers set curved and cornered and, at some point, twisted into loops, which she followed, per the directions Curly had given.

"Ridiculous," she muttered, stepping carefully between the plants as they formed a figure eight, a sign she recognized as meaning eternity. "I'm going nowhere at all."

She sighed deep and heavy. She was tired. She had barely slept the previous night and had been walking for so long she was starting to give up. But when she looked up next, there it was: an impossibly tall, narrow tree that should have been visible from anywhere on the island, though she had never seen it before.

The trunk went up so high she had to squint, and even then she saw only the sky and not the tops of the branches it held up. It was a kind of tree she had never seen before, and she prided herself on knowing every species that grew in Neverland. It looked as though it had been poured in thick ropes like taffy over the top of a tree mold and then left to dry.

She knew in her gut that this tree was not supposed to be here, maybe wasn't here at all. So she approached it with caution. "What are you?"

Under the wide branches, the air was cool and smelled like vanilla beans. Her stomach grumbled at the scent. She hadn't eaten in so long she could hardly remember her last meal. She put her hand over her noisy stomach as she turned, looking up at the thousands of leaves that made a moving canopy above her. And then she saw something in the grass.

"Oh, thank goodness." She fell to her knees and picked it up: a small bundle of fresh bright orange carrots, clean and perfect, the orange flesh topped with bushy green. Her mouth watered.

There was a movement by the trunk: a silver rabbit

hopped out from the shadows, his nose twitching. He'd obviously smelled the carrots, too. He took another jump in her direction, pausing and lifting a paw.

Tiger Lily knew rabbits were timid by nature. For him to be headed toward her, for him not to have turned and run away at the sight of her, he must be hungry, maybe as hungry as she was—maybe more. She sighed.

"You're hungry, too, eh?" She said it out loud. The animal sat up on his hind legs in response. There was something intelligent in his eyes, like he could understand her.

She looked at the carrots, shiny and crisp, and sighed again; then she held them out in his direction. "Okay, then, come and get them." She placed them back on the ground and stood slowly so he wouldn't be spooked. Just then, there was a low crackling sound, like the popping of a hundred bubbles, one after the other.

She turned to look at the tree, and at the base, where there had been nothing before, was a little door. Her stomach flipped itself into a knot, and suddenly she couldn't take another step. The door opened with a soft creak. And in the doorway, lit by candles burning within, stood the witch.

Tiger Lily swallowed the fear that had crept into her throat, shifted the weight of the book held between her right arm and her ribs, and headed for the door and whatever came next.

The witch was short, but not short enough to be called short. She had thick straight hair that shone silver in the moonlight and stayed silver in the shadows and hung over her shoulders. She was sturdy, as if planted in big boots, even though she was barefoot. She wore layers of skirts in different shades of red and had a necklace made of dried berries and toasted nuts looped twice around her neck.

"Welcome, welcome. You look like you're looking for me." She ushered the girl in and closed the door behind them.

Tiger Lily looked all around her. The room was circular, with its walls going up and up and up . . . probably all the way to the impossible top. Shelves lined the walls. They held mostly books but also jars and plants that had grown wild and lush out of their pots. Only candles and the soft glow of the moon far,

far above lit the space. There was a fireplace on the other side of the room, but the fire in it was small. A pot hung over it from a black rod, and good smells wafted from it. In front of it stood two comfy-looking chairs, one draped with a furry blanket. Many small rugs of all different shapes and colors covered the floor.

"I am. Looking for you, that is. I mean, I think I am." Tiger Lily couldn't concentrate. She was taking in all the colors and wonders around her. She saw sculptures, not unlike the ones in her village, here and there peering out from behind the plants. They appeared to watch her with their carved eyes and slight smiles. "Who are you, exactly?"

The woman laughed. The sound echoed and shook. It had weight. "Well, I'm LeeLee. Some call me the witch. But I'm just LeeLee."

"You're not a witch?" Tiger Lily wanted to take the words back as soon as she said them. They sounded wrong, like an insult. So she added, "No offense."

"Oh, no. No offense taken. I suppose I am a witch. But I am more than that. Just like you." She moved to a wooden table that looked like it had grown out of the dirt floor like a mushroom, the top covered with books and paper and quills. "You are more than just a seeker, are you not? You are also a great hunter and a fast rider and a loyal friend."

Tiger Lily nodded, then joined her at the table. The woman had a twinkle in her eye. Tiger Lily looked as shocked as she felt, her own eyes not twinkling, her lips parted with no words coming to them. Something tickled her ankle. She looked down. And then she jumped, pushing a stack of books off the table and onto the floor.

There was the rabbit from outside, rubbing his face against her leg. Only now he was bigger than any rabbit she'd ever seen. He was the same silver shade as LeeLee's hair and had paws as big as teacups. But the oddest thing was that from the top of his head grew a set of delicate antlers, with four points on each.

"Whoa," she whispered. She reached down and rested her hand on her shin, not sure if the creature was friendly. He might, after all, have a full set of sharp teeth in his twitching mouth. "This is the bunny from outside, I think. But I've never seen a rabbit like this before."

"I know," the witch answered. "He wanted to make a good impression." She leaned down and called under the table, "Didn't you, Ceese? Yes, you did."

The rabbit sniffed Tiger Lily's fingers and then hopped over to his master. Each bound sounded like an oar slapping on still water.

"Oh, there's a good boy," LeeLee cooed, scratching his head between the horns. "Yes, you are. Would you mind getting the tea ready?"

He bounded away, leaving Tiger Lily to wonder how a bunny could possibly prepare tea.

"Now then . . ." LeeLee clapped her hands. "What has brought you out to us today . . . ahhh . . ."

"Tiger Lily."

"Oh, yes, Tiger Lily, Tiger Lily." She looked around as if the room held an answer she was searching for. Finally, she raised a finger; she'd found whatever it was she was looking for. "Oh, I knew I knew that name. And you look so familiar. I know your great-great-grandmother. A phenomenal woman with a beautiful voice. Uncanny, really."

Tiger Lily was confused. She had never heard her grandmother sing. She would remember to ask her about it later if she managed to get out of this mess and see her family again.

"Now then, Tiger Lily. What do you need?" She didn't sound upset that a strange girl had shown up, uninvited, with a request. In fact, she sounded genuinely curious.

"Well . . ." Tiger Lily leaned in. The edge of the book she was still carrying hit the table, reminding her she had brought it.

"Oh, this is for you." She handed over the heavy volume.

LeeLee put both hands to her face. She was so excited. She reached out and grabbed the book as if it were a fragile thing that required great care. "Oh, my, what a perfect gift!"

She turned it toward her and examined the green cover. "*The Encyclopedia of Botanical Cures.* Oh, what a treat indeed!" She opened the cover right away and scanned the first pages.

Tiger Lily waited a moment. When it became clear the woman was not going to put the book away, she launched into her tale. She explained how she had discovered the pirates on the beach by accident, how they were after the Andon, a thing her fairy friend had never heard of and the mermaids told only the vaguest stories about. She said she had visited the Lost Boys, who had never even heard of an Andon but who had instead told her about the witch who might. All the while she spoke, the older woman flipped page after page in her new old book, smiling big and full as she did.

Tiger Lily paused. She wasn't sure if she should tell her about Sashi in the jar, about her own capture, about the mission she was on. She didn't want to get in trouble. But then she remembered that not telling was what had gotten her to this point.

"And the pirates, you see, they took my friend."

The woman glanced up. "The fairy?"

"Yes. And they grabbed me, too. I have until the sun rises again to get them the Andon, or they are going to toss her in the sea."

Saying it out loud brought tears to her eyes.

LeeLee reached across the table and took the girl's hand. "Oh, now, no need for tears. If anyone can do this, it's you. I know that about you already."

There was a clatter of porcelain. The woman looked down at her feet. "Ah! Our tea is ready."

"Wha . . ." Tiger Lily bent down. Sure enough, there was a silver tray set on the ground. On it were a chipped pot with steam rising out of the spout, two teacups, and a small tray of biscuits. "But . . . how?"

"Ceese likes making himself helpful. Don't you, boy?" She scratched the rabbit behind his ears, and he thumped his back leg so hard it shook the tray almost to ruin.

When the drinks had been poured and the biscuits nibbled and LeeLee had finally put Curly's book away, they began to talk in earnest.

The woman asked, "What exactly do you know of the Andon?"

It really wasn't very much, and Tiger Lily had started to calm down, so words came more easily now. "Well, the pirates—Jukes and Jolly are their names—they said it was a treasure, a shiny thing, and that it was the most valuable thing in all of Neverland, so powerful it may bring eternal youth. The mermaids said that it was called the Andon because it was named after a mermaid who swam away, maybe even taking it with her. And that's it. That's all. I have no idea what it even looks like, so I'm not sure how to go about finding it."

That was the truth, the most frustrating truth:

how could she find it when she didn't have the slightest idea what she was looking for?

"Well, now, I think you know exactly what it looks like." LeeLee winked at her. "But let's start at the beginning, shall we?"

The old woman stood, all her skirts gathering around her legs like petals folding in on a sleeping flower. "And the beginning is . . . everyone in this story so far is wrong, but also sort of right, too."

Oh, no, Tiger Lily thought. *More riddles.*

But there weren't riddles—there were answers, and LeeLee went through them, one by one.

"This thing, the Andon, is not named after anyone. It is named after what it is. You know how when something continues without end, people say 'it went on and on'?"

The girl nodded, taking another sip of her tea.

"Well, that's what this is. It goes on and on, and on, and on. . . . And so that is how it is called—the Andon. See? Simple." She clapped her hands, and many bracelets tinkled at her wrists. "We know that this Andon hasn't just been around forever; we know that it *is* forever."

"It's forever?"

"Exactly." LeeLee smiled at her as if she had said something exceptionally clever. "It is the thing that lets us live here in Neverland without end, the thing that allows those of us who don't choose otherwise to stay exactly the same."

"There is something that does that?" Tiger Lily had never thought about it before. It was just how things were, had always been.

"Yes, there is, and it is right here in this room."

Tiger Lily twisted and turned in her chair, looking all around her, up and down the long walls of books and trinkets. She saw a painting of a dog wearing a bonnet, a bowl that looked like it had been made by a child, and a glass vase full of birds folded out of paper. Could one of these things be the Andon?

LeeLee laughed. "It's not a thing, sweet girl. It's us! We carry the Andon"—she placed her own hand on her chest—"in here. It's the feeling you have in here. It's that feeling of magic and freedom and maybe even a bit of stubbornness that allows those in Neverland to never grow up or old or, in some cases, any older than they already are." She tossed her silver hair over her shoulder.

"So, wait, it's not a treasure—it's a feeling?" Tiger

Lily was getting dizzy. It was hard to get clear and confused at the same time.

"Almost. It's more of a philosophy. You understand philosophy?"

"Isn't that the word for the things we believe?"

LeeLee gave her another smile. "Clever girl. But again, sort of. It's a yes and a no answer. It is both what we believe and the ways in which we think to get to those beliefs. It's like the rules we give ourselves, the pathways we carve out for our thoughts to travel in order to get to different beliefs."

Tiger Lily imagined little trails mapped out on the inside of her head. "I get it. So the Andon is the philosophy we share that lets us live on and on and on?"

Now LeeLee jumped up and down in short little hops that set Ceese jumping in circles around the table. "You got it!"

Tiger Lily couldn't help laughing. The woman's joy was contagious. She watched her and her pet, who was really more of a true friend, as they celebrated. She moved her shoulders in a kind of dance, to join in on the fun, but then she stopped.

"Wait, what does this mean for the treasure hunt?"

The more she thought about it, the more her old

fears returned and filled her muscles. She stood. "If I go back there with some story about pathways in our heads and not gold or some jeweled goblet, the pirates will never believe me!"

LeeLee was at her side in a flash. "Oh, no, don't worry so. Worry doesn't help things. It just makes it harder to think of the answers. Come now, finish your tea."

She guided the girl to sit back down and handed her the cup. Then she returned to her own seat and waited until Tiger Lily had taken a sip and a deep breath.

"Now, here's what I know. I know that things happen for a reason. That's another one of my own philosophies. And I think there are no accidents. You found those pirates because you were supposed to. Who knows? Maybe you are the only person here who can handle this mess. And I know that you are going to use your own philosophies to figure it out."

The woman sat back and finished off her cup. She picked a biscuit off the tray and took a big bite. Her eyes got wide. She turned to her pet, who waited by her chair. "Oh, Ceese, you've really outdone yourself this time."

Even now, in the midst of trying to put out the

fires her worry was setting, Tiger Lily couldn't help being astounded. "The rabbit baked the biscuits?"

"When you come back another day, Ceese will show you his true talents in the kitchen. We'll have ourselves a real feast! Bring your grandmother with you. I'd love to visit with Sage again."

Sage. It had been a long time since she had heard anyone use her grandmother's given name. It made her happy to think of being here with both LeeLee and her grandmother. Oh, the stories she would hear! But right now Tiger Lily had work to do.

She cleared her throat. "So . . . just to get this straight: I need to figure out a way to hand over a treasure that isn't an object or worth any coins to a couple of pirates who only want coins?"

"Exactly!" LeeLee clapped. "That's exactly right. See? I knew you would figure this out."

"But . . ." Tiger Lily started. But the woman was already up and pulling out a ladder on wheels, the tallest ladder Tiger Lily had ever seen, to put away her new treasured book. "Help me with this, Ceese. I need to get up to the herb section."

After they had finished their snack and said their goodbyes, Tiger Lily stood at the door.

"You ready to finish your adventure?" LeeLee asked, brushing crumbs off the girl's shirt like a fussy auntie.

Tiger Lily sighed. "I'm not sure. I still don't know what to do. I mean, there is no treasure. That means I have nothing to bring to the pirates."

"Well, now, I think one of those pathways in your brilliant head might lead you to the right solution after all." She tapped the girl's forehead. "Have faith in yourself. I do."

They embraced; then Tiger Lily bent to give Ceese, the baking, tea-serving, antlered rabbit, a quick scratch that set his leg thumping. And then she was off.

At the first blue bloom on the trail that would lead her back to her horse, she turned. "Can I come back and visit you again soon? I mean, even if I don't have a book?"

LeeLee smiled, showing all her teeth. "My girl, you can always come back and visit without a book now that you know where you're going."

She held the door and waited for her enormous bunny to bound inside. "That's it, Ceese. Let's go get some knitting done."

"Knitting," Tiger Lily said in awe "How in the world . . . ?"

The door closed, and the tree darkened, the moon shifting away from its branches.

Tiger Lily turned back to the path, with the magical tree behind her. She felt a bit taller, a little wiser, and a lot more confident. Yes, LeeLee was right; she supposed she did know where she was going. And even better, thanks to LeeLee, the witch who was so much more than a witch, a plan was beginning to form in her mind. Tiger Lily knew there was no treasure, but the pirates had no idea. And surely, she could use that to her advantage.

Chapter Nineteen

As far as Tiger Lily could tell, the only difference between a child and a grown-up—besides the size of clothes you needed to make—was just how useful you were in an emergency. Kids looked for an adult when things went bad. But adults? They looked to themselves and maybe, sometimes, to each other. But then, they didn't really have any choice, did they?

She decided now was the time to think like an adult. Because, well, she didn't really have any choice.

The walk back from the witch's house was not as long as the walk there had been. She did it in a kind of trance, stepping carefully and thinking hard, not bothering to try to take note of things around her, like distance and landmarks. As she walked over each blue bloom, it closed up tight and then retreated into the soil from which it had sprung. The path was disappearing as she walked it. She realized that this had been her path all along, made specifically for her and this journey.

"Oh, LeeLee"—she smiled, talking out loud into the darkness—"I will definitely be back to see you."

She started her planning by listing the facts as they were. Sashi was being held by two pirates who had her knife, and a cutlass, and maybe more that she hadn't seen. They wanted a treasure that didn't exist. If she was lucky, the crows would find her grandmother. But even if they did, Tiger Lily had to hurry. She only had until the midday meal to bring this imaginary treasure to the pirates and then hope that they kept their rotten word and returned Sashi unharmed.

That was a lot. But she wasn't giving up. Not now. Not on her friend. Not on herself. She would find a way to use what she had to rescue Sashi. She had the Lost Boys, with their slingshots and one bow and sharpened sticks. She had her grandmother's horse.

And she had her mind, full of a thousand different paths heading in all directions.

She arrived back at the Lost Boys' place just as the sky was unwrapping itself from its heavy blanket of night. There she found all four of them curled up like a pile of puppies in the middle of the field, just about where she had begun her walk. She was quiet, not wanting to wake them. She herself felt completely refreshed, as if she had rested well and slept deep and was now ready to begin. And she *was* ready to begin.

The sky turned to a bright pink with smears of happy orange. Her shadow crept along the ground and fell over the sleeping children. Curly, roused by some shift in the atmosphere, sat up and blinked at her. She smiled; then her smile faltered when she saw the early sky.

"Pink is not good in the morning."

"I know the old rhyme," Tiger Lily responded. "Pink sky at night, sailor's delight. Pink sky at morning, sailor's warning."

"Yes, that's the one." Curly yawned. "Peter told it to us. He swears by it."

"Good thing we're not sailors, then."

"We need the shiniest, most special thing we can find," she told the Lost Boys once they had all woken. "Something that looks like a pirate would sell his soul for it."

"A pirate would sell his soul for an empty crab leg," Nibs murmured.

"Something rarer than a crab leg, then," she answered. "Or at least something that *seems* rarer."

They were all sitting in Fort Fierce, legs crossed, fists under their chins, doing the hard work of thinking.

"What about a bog bully?" Twin One shouted, excited by her own idea.

"Mmmm, I don't think they would think a giant swamp snail is all that special," Tiger Lily replied gently.

"Then they're dumber than they look," One replied.

Tiger Lily tousled her hair. "Good thinking, though."

"Oh, I found a rock that looks like a finger!" shouted out Nibs, his own finger raised in the air.

"Think more . . . mannish," Tiger Lily said.

"Could be a man's finger," Nibs said.

"No, no. I mean think of things that would have come here from somewhere else. Someplace through the stars."

"Like London town, where Peter is always going?" Two asked.

"Yes! Exactly!"

They all settled back into silence, thinking. Finally, Curly slapped her hands down on her thighs. "Well, if we need something from a place where Peter is always going, then I think we'd better look in Peter's room."

No one said a word. The twins looked at each other and then at the floorboards.

"But Peter don't like us going in his room, never mind touching his things," Nibs said, his voice barely a whisper.

"Listen, Peter ain't here, and I am," Curly said, standing. She threw her shoulders back and tried to look important. "And besides, Peter is a lot of things, but he is and always has been a good friend. Tiger Lily is his friend, and if he was here, he'd give her his own bleeding heart if she asked for it."

She sounded surer than she looked.

"Yuck," the twins said together.

"It's an expression, guys," Curly clarified. "Besides, what would Tiger Lily do with a squishy wet thing like a heart?"

This made them giggle and make fake puking noises at each other.

"You're right, Curly." Tiger Lily started through the hatch, her feet reaching for the top step nailed to the trunk. "I'm going to the hideout, and I'm going to get something from the stars." She paused. "In case, you know, anyone wants to come help."

The Lost Boys all looked at each other and then away. No one was brave enough to go against Peter's wishes. Curly spoke up. "I'll go, then. It was my idea, after all. And Lost Boys ain't ascared of nothing."

"And I'm not a Lost Boy," Tiger Lily chimed in. "So I don't have to follow the rules."

"But, Lily," Two said, "o' course you're a Lost Boy, silly."

That made her smile as they climbed down the tree.

Peter Pan's room was not as messy as one would expect. There was a nest of blankets in all shapes and sizes, which could never be made up to look decent. But other than that, his things were all neatly stacked and carefully placed. They were laid out on the floor, on a three-legged table held up by a stack of impossibly balanced rocks, and across an old chair, but still, they were *neatly* laid there. There was a huge hole in the wall that looked out over all Neverland, and Tiger Lily stopped to gaze out for a moment before pulling her focus back to the mission.

"Okay, let's see what we've got," Tiger Lily whispered. She wasn't sure why she was whispering, but there was something about being in another person's private space without them there that made her feel like she had to be as small as possible.

Tiger Lily looked around. There were a lot of things from around Neverland here: rocks, branches, even a small dish of colorful jewels that looked like they might have come from a mermaid. She picked up a bundle of feathers that had been carefully tied together with a bit of old rope. It kind of resembled a figure, like a simple doll. For some reason, that broke her heart a little. She placed the feather doll back carefully and sorted through a pile of clothes to see if there was anything hiding in the stack—maybe a necklace or a hat that could do the trick. Nothing. Next she went to the window ledge. There she found the kinds of things she was looking for.

"There are a few potential Andons here," she said.

"Really?" Curly answered. "Well, pick one and let's get out of here."

But she wanted to browse them first to make sure she could come up with the story that would make the object a treasure before carrying it off into potential battle. Looking through his things, she thought Peter seemed more childlike than ever before. She could forgive him his bragging as she looked at the odd possessions of a lonely boy.

"Why are you scared of Peter?" she asked, knowing it was kind of a mean thing to bring up.

"I ain't scared of Peter," Curly answered, more loudly than a whisper, which made her look at the door. That quick glance betrayed the lie in her words. "Well, I mean, I'm not scared, but I am kind of nervous like."

"What do you mean?" Tiger Lily picked up a long piece of leather with a line of holes and a metal clasp on the end. Next she picked up a small silver needle, the kind she made out of bone to sew even stitches in soft hide.

"I mean, I don't worry that he might get mad. I worry that he might not come back." Curly sounded embarrassed. "We Lost Boys, we only really have each other. And Peter? He's the one that made us who we are."

Tiger Lily thought she understood. Peter Pan was like a parent in this house. An irresponsible, refusing-to-grow-up, childish parent. But still, she understood.

"He's your thread," she remarked, still holding the needle.

"Thread?"

"Yeah, he's the thing that holds you all together." She placed the needle back on the sill and picked up a large wooden spoon with flowers burned into the handle. There was a frayed ribbon tied around the top. It must have been black-and-white gingham once, but now it was splotchy gray.

"I suppose that's true," Curly responded. "He is a kind of thread."

"Oh, what about this?" Tiger Lily interrupted, holding out a small metal box. It fit in the palm of one hand, and there was a little knob sticking out of the side. Curly crossed the room and took it gently from her. She fidgeted with the knob and found that it turned. So she turned it, round and round, until it wouldn't turn anymore. Then she released it.

Nothing happened. They looked at each other, their

eyebrows pulled down. Tiger Lily took it back and flipped it upside down to examine the bottom. She stuck her fingernail under the crack around the edge, and the top opened up. And then there was music—tinny and low, but music nonetheless.

"What is it?" Curly asked, whispering again.

Their heads were bent close together as they listened, watching the knob unwind itself with peals of echoey music.

Tiger Lily whispered her answer. "That, my very good friend, is our Andon."

Chapter
Twenty

I t was an older crow who found Tiger Lily's
people. They were way out on the southern tip
of Neverland on a peninsula they'd never camped
on before, as far as he knew, and he knew pretty far.

The fish this year were plentiful and wily. They'd
led the people on a merry chase before swimming in
vast circles, creating cyclones in the water. Old Crow
found them because he had been listening, really listening, the kind of listening that came with age. He had
also brought with him something that would help the
human understand his message. He carried it clasped
in his claw, folded close to his downy chest.

The other feathered searchers had shot out of the

field like soft arrows, already fighting among themselves about who was the fastest, who would be the
first to spot the traveling village.

They are on a fishing trip, the girl had said. So the
first thing Old Crow did was head to the water. He flew
high but slow, gliding on a current when he caught
one, resting against the cushion of moving air. There
was no sense in racing the others; he wasn't in a race.
They were fools to compete when there was no need for
competition. Younger crows forgot that, always trying
to be the best. Old Crow preferred to be the smartest.

Once he was way up, it was easy to trace the line
where the land met the sea. He followed it like a ribbon that had fallen on the ground. After a while, he
closed his eyes on and off. Because this wasn't about
finding moving dots and hoping it was them. No, this
was about the fish.

Old Crow knew the people went out when the
whitefish ran close to the island. He knew then that
he needed two things to find them: his sense of smell
and his sense of hearing.

So while the others were off chasing an imaginary
win or trying to stay low and jumping at every movement in the woods, Old Crow was up high, floating

on the breezes, smelling and listening. And eventually, it paid off.

He had only been out for about two hours when the air began to gather a kind of static around its edges. It was a disturbance of sound—small jabs at first; then they knitted together to form a prickly sheet, then finally burst into a cacophony. Only one thing made a noise like that: seagulls. He focused on what was sure to be the center of the screams, then tilted his wings and pointed himself straight for it.

Old Crow sighed, wincing as he cut through a swarm of gulls. He was a quiet black visitor in a sea of gray squabblers. He didn't bother excusing himself as he worked his way through them. They barely noticed him as it was.

And then he saw what he had come for: the girl's people, quiet and careful, doing their work with practiced ease, ignoring the screaming battle happening right above their heads. Old Crow was smooth and focused, making several passes over the peninsula, going out over the small fishing boats and looking for the one who would welcome his message. Finally, he found her, sitting on the shore, busy with the work of preparing the caught fish to be brought back to the smokehouse.

These people always impressed Old Crow. They only took what they needed. They followed the rules of the seasons and took care of the land so that there were always more than enough animals and other food to eat. And they had ways of preparing the meat, like the smokehouse, so that it wouldn't rot and waste before they had a chance to eat it.

Old Crow swooped low and hopped once, twice, three times before he came to a stop right near her foot. She didn't look up. There were too many birds to notice just one, especially a quiet one who didn't need to be shooed away from the catch. He hopped closer and tapped his beak on the soft leather of her moccasin, stopping himself from pecking at the shiny beadwork that caught his eye. He was, after all, a crow.

"Oh, hello there, old fellow. You out fishing, too?" She smiled at him, a knife in one hand, a half-gutted fish in the other. "There's plenty for everyone."

Yes, he knew this one. This was the one who had fed his family for generations. And not just scraps. She left whole cobs of corn, the ripest of ground fruit. He cawed once in response and moved closer.

The woman chuckled, then looked more closely at him. "I know you, don't I?"

He cawed again. Just once, so that she understood it as an answer and not just a sound.

"I see. We do know each other, you and I." She winked at him. The she cut a long strip of fresh fish off and handed it to him. "Are you hungry?"

Oh, he wanted that fish. It was cold from the sea and clean from her knife work. But taking it would mean he was just being a hungry bird. And he was a hungry bird. But more than that, right now he was a messenger. So he stayed still, not stepping back out of fear of a human's touch, not stepping forward to beg for her food. Instead, he stamped his foot on the ground and cawed again.

She pulled her hand back and tilted her head. "What is it? Are you all right?"

He walked in a quick circle on the rocky ground, showing he was fine.

"Are you tired?"

He flapped his wings hard and fast while standing in one spot. He was not tired.

Now she was intrigued. And when she put aside her work and the fish was quickly snatched up by one of the screamy dive-bombers, she barely took notice.

"What is it, then?"

This was the moment he hopped forward, onto her moccasin, then up on her knee, and dropped what he had carried with him into her hand. It was a strand of hair from the girl's head. He had pulled it free himself back at the field, quick and hard so it wouldn't hurt.

The woman picked it out of her palm with the other hand, then stretched it between her fingers. She held it up to the sun and then brought it close to her face.

"Tiger Lily," she whispered.

He jumped from her lap and flew circles over her head, cawing like mad, like a well-mannered seagull.

"This is Tiger Lily's hair," she called up to him. "Is she okay?"

He flew back down to her knee and stared her straight in the eye. He barely drew breath, concentrating, looking at her the way he looked when his own children were taking their first flight: nervous, worried. He hoped she saw it there, in his dark eyes, the anxiety that announced that something was wrong.

She looked, really looked. The kind of looking that came with age. And then she stood up fast. The slab of wood she was using as a cutting board clattered to the rocks at her feet. She had seen the word he carried in his eyes, and that word was *emergency*. She knew it as sure as if he had said it out loud. She had to move, and she had to move now.

"Gee! Gee, get me a horse!" she yelled. "Oh, I knew I shouldn't have ridden in the cart. I knew I should have insisted on taking my own steed!" She was angry, but only with herself. Every other edge in her voice was from worry.

The boy ran over. "What's that, Grandmother?"

"I said, get me a horse. The fastest here. I need to go . . . now."

"What's wrong?" he asked, already walking backward toward the temporary camp to do her bidding. Even in her advanced age, she was not a woman to be ignored. She was a woman who rarely gave orders, and when she did, they were to be followed.

"I have to get back. It's Tiger Lily, and she needs me."

Chapter Twenty—One

Tiger Lily rode the mare with restraint. "Save all that speed, girl. We might need it."

She sat tall in the saddle, keeping the horse to an even trot. Every now and then, she looked into the tree line to her right. There she would see the Lost Boys, traveling as they always did, on foot, running and jumping. Only now they left out their usual yelling and whooping. They moved quickly and silently. They stayed so close that she felt like she had grown four new shadows. This made her proud: she had managed to teach them, and they were doing great.

Every time a bird flew overhead, she caught her

breath. Was it a crow bringing word of her grand-mother? But then it was just an eagle pulling a weasel across the sky toward her nest, or a cluster of song-birds composing a new melody.

You've got this, she reminded herself. *Everything is going to be fine . . . just fine.*

But when she got to the border of the Hilly Woods, all her good thoughts evaporated. She brought the horse to a full stop. Suddenly, the trees seemed menacing, like skeletons with reaching arms and sharp claws. The shadows connected so that there was only solid dark ahead. The sounds of bugs and small animals grew to an eerie wail. Everything inside her was telling her to turn back, that only danger lay ahead.

A small whistle broke through her growing panic. She looked over and saw Curly standing on a rock so that she was taller than the cedars along the perimeter. Curly smiled.

You've got this, she mouthed. *We are with you.*

Tiger Lily smiled. Seeing that her friends believed in her made her believe in herself.

She took a deep breath, sat up very straight, and clicked her tongue. The mare took her first steps into the woods, and soon Tiger Lily was in the solid dark.

Bill Jukes stood with Tiger Lily's knife tucked into the waistband of his pants. "Well, well, you ain't one what believes in being early, are ya?"

Jolly stood behind him, holding both a long cutlass and the jar. Inside the jar, Sashi fluttered and jumped, motioning for Tiger Lily to get out of there. At the same time, there was real relief on her face: someone had come for her.

"You gave me a deadline, and I kept to that," Tiger Lily said. She dismounted a few yards away from the men. She patted the horse on her nose to let her know she was to stay and took one step forward. "I'm here on time. No sense in hanging around with you lot any longer than I have to."

Jukes put his mitt of a hand to his chest. "Ow. You break me old heart with that kind of talk." He was teasing her, but Jolly actually did look a little bit hurt.

"Well," Jukes said, "where is it, then?"

Trying to look confident, Tiger Lily planted her feet firmly in the sand and rested her hands on her hips. "I'll be taking the fairy first."

"Oh, you will, will ya," he scoffed, looking back at

Jolly, who took the cue and barked out a short laugh.

She stayed calm and focused . . . on the outside, at least. "Yes. I want to make sure she is safe before I hand over such a vast and powerful treasure."

At the word *treasure*, the pirates' eyes got large. They were trained dogs hearing their favorite word. Jukes grabbed the jar from his partner's hand and held it up. Sashi braced herself against the curved glass to stay upright with the movement.

"Here, you can see she's all right. It's bloody glass, isn't it? You can see right through it." He shook it a bit. "See? She's right here and she's standing and everything. Raised enough noise last night tryna escape, too."

Of course she did, Tiger Lily thought, stifling a smile.

"Why don't we split the difference?" she suggested. "Put the jar down halfway between us. That way I know you don't mean to hold on to her."

He scratched at his chin with the back of his hand. "Well, then, put the treasure in the middle, too. So we know you ain't meaning to hold on to it."

"Yeah," Jolly echoed. "Good thinkin', Jukes."

"Shut it, Jolly."

Tiger Lily sighed, shaking her head. "You know,

Chapter Twenty-One

I don't think you two know much about the Andon after all."

"Whaddya mean?" Jukes was insulted. "We do too."

"Really?" She crossed her arms over her chest. "It just seems weird, then, that you'd wanna waste time arguing, knowing what you know. . . ."

"What's she talkin' about?" Jolly loud-whispered.

"I said, shut it," Jukes hissed over his shoulder. He cleared his throat, even paced a little. "Listen, I'm thinkin' you don't know what you have. So just to be sure, why don't you tell us what you think you know, and we'll tell you if yous is right?"

Tiger Lily pretended to consider this request, as if it wasn't obvious they were clueless. "Well, okay, then. I heard that the Andon is a secret philosophy. And you know what that means?"

"O' course we do," Jukes spat. "What do you think that means?" He leaned in to listen very carefully.

"It means the person who possesses it can control anything and everything. It's the most powerful thing there is."

Jukes considered this, his head tipped to the side. "Okay, then, missus. If this is true, then why isn't you using it on us right now?"

"Oh," she said, "that's simple. Only the bravest and . . . uh, the tallest of men can possess the Andon."

Jukes stood very straight now, to his full height. "Well, then, I guess you is too small and too much of a coward, then?"

Tiger Lily kept her cool. She pretended to be disappointed. "Yes, I suppose I am. But then, you knew all this. That's why you had me go and get it. You already knew I wouldn't be able to use it."

Jukes smiled. "That is right-o."

"Wow, you are so smart," Jolly gushed. "I mean, I knew you was smart by pirate standards, but this is just amazing, Jukesy."

"Well, some of us have many gifts." Jukes swaggered now, his chest puffed out like a bird's. "I am one o' those lucky fellas."

"Guess I'm just surprised that you'd be worried about, well, anything," said Tiger Lily with a shrug. "We all know that as soon as you have the Andon, I won't be able to pull any tricks anyway. Even if I wanted to, which I don't. I just want to get my little friend and get out of here."

Maybe Jukes *was* smart by pirate standards, because

he didn't jump to the bait right away. Instead, he paused, narrowing his eyes at the girl.

"I want proof," he finally said.

"Proof?"

"Yeah. Proof. How do I even know you got the right one, the right Andon?"

"Well, there's only one." Tiger Lily stalled.

"Yeah, yeah. Enough." Jukes cracked his knuckles, making her nervous. "No more talk. Just get the thing and hand it over."

"F-f-fairy in the middle first . . . please." His hand curling into a tight fist brought fear into her voice.

"All right, why not?" He carried the jar to the middle ground between them on the beach and then slowly backed away. "Toss it over, then."

Tiger Lily walked back to the mare and retrieved a sack tied to her saddle. She loosened the strings and carefully brought out Peter Pan's music box. She held it in both hands, walking slowly, as if it were something very powerful indeed.

"That's it?" Jukes sounded disappointed by the simple metal box.

"It's bee-you-tiful," whispered an impressed Jolly.

"Careful now." Tiger Lily bent and set it down beside the jar very slowly and with great care. She paused to wink at Sashi, who looked as confused now as she was scared. "It's more valuable than anything else that was ever made."

Once it was in the sand, she stepped back and blew air out of her mouth in a loud puff. "All right, then, go ahead."

Jukes paused. He looked a bit nervous himself. "Jolly, be a mate and go fetch it."

"Sure thing, boss." Jolly stumbled forward, kicking up sand. He stuck his tongue out, concentrating as he bent and carefully lifted the music box, then turned back. A few steps from Jukes, he tripped, and the box went flying, but Jukes caught it.

"Good catch," Jolly sighed. He got only a growl in response.

Jukes looked at all sides, then flipped it upside down. "Uh, remind me, how does this thing work again?"

"Still testing me, eh?" Tiger Lily kept up the ruse. "You are a crafty one. You know you have to wind the little knob on the side until it won't wind anymore, then you open the lid."

"That's right," he said, chuckling. "Very good."

He wound the knob. It took him a minute with his clumsy fingers, not used to delicate things, to manage the small latch on the lid. When the music started playing, he was so surprised he almost dropped it.

"And now you wait a minute, and then speak your wish, loud and clear, and it will happen," Tiger Lily said. She didn't wait for him to ask for the next step. "And start small. Start with controlling things smaller and more cowardly than you, until the Andon gets to trust you, and then you can ask for bigger things."

The pirate looked like a giant child, his face full of wonder. The music enchanted him, so soft and bright at the same time. Finally, he closed his eyes and shouted, "I wish for the girl to dance."

Ugh. Tiger Lily scowled. *Of all the stupid . . .*

But then, her eyes wide with surprise, she raised her hands slowly, as if they were out of her control, and held them above her head. She pulled one leg up and then turned a graceful spin on her toes. She kicked out and jumped and spun again and again, all the while looking shocked at her own movements.

Jolly clapped his hands, laughing loudly. "She's doing it! She's doing it!"

"Now I wish for the girl to . . . to stand on her

head." Jukes smiled at this request and watched her expectantly.

Oh, no . . .

But Tiger Lily dropped to her hands and knees, looking up at him with that same expression of wonder. Then she put her head into the sand and lifted her legs up. She flexed her stomach muscles and straightened her legs, keeping her ankles locked together, trying to maintain balance.

"Make her do more, more!" Jolly was jumping about like a toddler.

She let her legs drop and rolled back to standing. "You have your proof. Now, please, let us go."

"No, I want to make sure. Andon . . ."

Uh-oh, she thought. Who knew what he was going to ask for now?

"I wish for the very trees to shiver at my power."

The three of them—four including Sashi, who watched from her jar—looked around at the trees surrounding them. Nothing happened.

"You have to be louder for bigger requests," Tiger Lily said.

"Trees! I said *shake!*" This time he shouted.

And after a few seconds, the two trees directly behind Tiger Lily did begin to shake. They bounced their branches until leaves fell.

Tiger Lily was impressed. She just hoped the men didn't notice the small bodies jumping and pushing with all their might up in the branches. But fortunately, the pirates were too busy celebrating. They danced their own little jig around each other, linking arms and kicking up their heels.

"We could take the ship with this!"

"Make Hook walk the plank!"

"Make 'em all walk the plank!"

She rolled her eyes. Pirates were such terrible friends.

"So we'll be going, then," she said. "No use for us anymore."

She stealthily ran forward and grabbed the jar, then rushed back toward the horse as quickly as she could.

"Andon!" Jukes shouted.

"Ah, maybe you shouldn't ask so much right away; it might be tired," Tiger Lily said. He was getting out of control, and she still had to get off the beach and to a safe distance.

"Nonsense, the music still plays. I have more wishes," he retorted. *"Andon, I wish it would rain gold!"*

Oh, no, Tiger Lily thought. She held the jar tight and broke into a run, trying to make it to her horse before the pirates realized the truth.

Chapter Twenty–Two

Tiger Lily's grandmother rode hard and fast on her borrowed steed. She burst out of the fish camp without hesitation and headed straight for home. Tiger Lily needed her. There was nothing in this world that could stop her. Old Crow followed her from the sky, cawing every now and then so that she knew he was still with her.

She leaned forward, lowering her torso to the animal's back, and held tight to the reins. This cut back on wind resistance and the jostling to her bones. It also reminded her of years gone by, when she rode every day. Sage was a master hunter, the best in her village. A part of her success was her speed; no one was faster. But more than that, it was her gratitude. Sage spent time with the animal after she took it down. She thanked the creature for its sacrifice so that her family and neighbors could eat, could have hide for clothes and bones for tools. She sang her gratitude across the fields and into the trees. It was a beautiful song that charmed the birds and pulled the underground dwellers out of their holes to listen. It was an honor to fall to her arrows.

But the day had come when Sage wanted more than the hunt. She wanted a partner, and then she wanted a child. After that, the day came when she wanted to see what her children's children would be like, to help train them to hunt and to sing. It was a great joy to do this work, this passing on of sound and movement. To watch the success of the people, the ways in which they prospered, while making sure they never forgot their past? That was the thing she was most grateful for.

She never regretted her decisions, any one, to grow older, to see the generations unfold. If she had never aged, she wouldn't have become a mother and Tiger Lily would never have been born to her daughter. That day had been one of the best days in memory.

It had been a long, wet spring that year, and summer had just started to make itself known with a hotter sun that stayed in the sky a little longer each day. Sage had been summoned to the home of Rose at daybreak. She had had a long night laboring, and the baby was ready to come into the world.

As her ancestor and relative, Sage was the first to hold the newborn. The baby had a head of thick hair and tiny fingers that were already reaching to grasp.

"She's looking for her reins," Sage joked, amazed at the tiny bundle settling against her chest. "This girl will need a good horse."

The baby was folded up, the way newborns were when they first came into the world. Later, when she was relaxed enough to take up more space, Sage saw how long her limbs were, how delicate her fingers.

"She will be tall and strong," Sage said.

She also noticed a sprinkling of spots dusting her cheeks, beauty marks, brown on brown.

"She looks like the lilies that grow along the forest edge," Sage remarked.

And for a while, that was what she was called: Lily. It wasn't until she had been running around the village and received her beloved Pony that her full personality emerged. Yes, she was tall; yes, she was a natural rider; but more than that, she was brave. It was the kind of bravery Sage knew would have to be tempered with wisdom so that the girl didn't become reckless. So Sage kept her close, telling her stories, teaching her to listen.

And the girl did listen, following her beloved grandmother around, her head bent toward the ground to concentrate on the words. This posture, face turned toward the ground, plus her natural drive toward adventure and her ferocity in protecting her friends, was why her name changed. She was still a child when she became Tiger Lily, and Tiger Lily she had been ever since. Sage had named her both times. The girl was special to her. She was special to everyone the way young people are, but there was something about this one that made Sage feel like maybe she could move on to whatever came next after old age. This one made her feel that the circle was complete, that she could go to her rest. If she didn't get such a kick out of watching Tiger Lily grow, she might have already gone on. This girl reminded Sage of herself, only the best version of herself she could imagine.

And now she was in trouble. Nothing in creation could have kept the old woman from getting to her girl.

Sage got to the village in record time, taking the horse directly to Tiger Lily's place.

"Tiger Lily," she called out.

There was no answer. The silence made the woman shiver. Panic, hot and cold at the same time, poured into her bones.

"Tiger Lily, where are you?"

A small boy, oblivious to the horse and rider turning to look in all directions, skipped across the field. He was wet from an early swim, and cupped a large frog in his hands.

"You," Sage yelled to him. He was so shocked by her booming voice that he dropped the frog, which gleefully hopped off, back toward the water. "Where is Tiger Lily?"

It took him a moment to recognize Sage, his own relative, atop a silver horse he knew belonged to one of the younger hunters. "The Lost Boys had a message for you."

"Well, what is it?" She wasn't cross with him; she was just out of time. She knew it. She could feel it in her stomach. Something was happening, and she had to get to Tiger Lily as soon as possible.

"Um, the boy said . . ." The child tapped his nose with a finger while he thought. "I can't remember. Something with pirates . . ."

"Pirates?" That was about as bad as it could be. "So where is she? At Skull Rock?"

He closed his eyes, deep in thought, then snapped his fingers. "Nope. She's out by the beach."

Sage sighed, deep and long. "My boy, there are many beaches." She tried her calm voice.

"Hmmmmm . . ." He tapped at his nose. "I think . . . I think . . ."

"Yes?" She was leaning over in her saddle toward him.

Just then the frog he had been carrying hopped between them. "Froggy!" he yelled, and was off on a merry chase.

"Really should have picked a different messenger there, Lost Boys," she said under her breath. It wasn't the little guy's fault. She was about to call out to him again when there came the sound of galloping hooves from behind. She turned; there was Pony, having recovered and galloped from the meadow. Sage dismounted and clicked her tongue, and Pony ran straight to her.

"Pony? What are you doing here?"

He seemed frantic, rearing back and kicking his front legs.

"You can feel it, too, eh?" she asked him when he nudged her hands with his nose. "She needs us, and I need you. You need to find her, boy."

If anything could take her directly to her granddaughter, it was Pony. Tiger Lily and her horse shared a special bond, a connection that could not be replicated. He knew her movements and habits better than anything in Neverland. So Sage wound her hands tight around the reins, and the second she was settled, Pony was off. She narrowed her eyes as the landscape sped past them.

"Hold on, my girl. We're coming."

High above, a single black bird had multiplied into a collection of shapes flying together, dark against the bright sky.

Chapter Twenty-Three

Tiger Lily had one hand on the mare and the other wrapped around the jar when Bill Jukes saw her.

"Wait right there," he shouted, tossing the knife in the air, then catching it. At that moment, the music box reached the end of its cycle and the music stopped. "Where d'ya think you're off to, then?"

"Home," she said, but it came out like a question.

"No, no, no . . ." Jukes took another step toward her. "Not just yet."

"But you got the Andon, and you got your proof . . . the dancing, the trees. . . ."

"If that's all it can do, then I think maybe I got a bum deal, don't you?"

Tiger Lily was distracted by a small tapping coming from the jar. She looked down. Sashi was pushing against the lid, banging on the metal surface. *Of course!* Tiger Lily could release her. She took her hand off the horse and placed it on the lid.

"Now hold on!" Jukes said. So did Jolly, who joined him, with the cutlass held tight in his hand. "Don't you be getting no ideas there, missus."

"But why?" She was starting to get frantic. "Why does she have to suffer? You got your treasure!"

"I didn't get my last wish," Jukes replied. "How do I know you weren't playing at being controlled?"

"What about the trees?"

Jukes considered this, finally snorting his dissatisfaction. "Coulda been the wind."

"Pretty good timing for the wind . . ." She hadn't moved her hand off the lid yet. Maybe if she distracted them . . . "And besides, you didn't get your last wish because the music ended, and that's where the magic comes from—the song. You should wind it up and try again."

"Ah, this blasted thing. *So* finicky and whatnot." He

handed over the knife to Jolly and instructed, "Keep an eye on her, you."

Jukes found the knob and began winding. Tiger Lily shifted her glance between Jolly and the trees, watching for an opportunity. All she needed was a moment of distraction and she could make a break for it. But for once, he was focused.

"There we are," Jukes cried out as the music began to play. "All right, then, let's try that again, shall we?"

Jolly smiled and shifted his weight from one foot to the other in time with the little melody.

"Andon, I demand the sky rain gold!"

Tiger Lily's heart was beating so loud it filled her ears. Each second stretched out, filled with danger and fear in equal measure. Both men lifted their faces toward the sky, waiting for the riches that would soon fall down all around them. And in that moment, with their eyes turned away to the clouds, Tiger Lily tightened her grip on the jar, twisted her wrist, and popped the lid off.

The two girls locked eyes, and Tiger Lily nodded. Sashi nodded back, then crouched down low, her hand on the ground near her foot, her eyes narrowed, and her whole body tense.

Ziiing!

The fairy shot out the opening as quick as she could, flying past her friend's face and into the sky in a flurry of tinkling bells and gossamer wings. Tiger Lily dropped the empty jar in the sand and, in one smooth movement, pulled herself onto her horse.

"Hey!" Jolly yelled. "She's gettin' away!"

Jukes dropped the music box. The song still played from the ground, but it sounded warped, uneven in a way.

Just then, something heavy landed in the sand, directly between the girl and the pirates. Then another, this time close to Jolly's bare foot. He stepped back and inspected the object. He squinted with his bad eyes, then gasped.

"It can't be. . . ."

"What?" Jukes asked.

"It's working," Jolly yelled. "Boss, it's rainin' gold!"

Another chunk landed in the dirt, and another. They were getting dangerously close to the men, flying through the air at great speeds. A large piece hit Jolly directly in his stomach.

"*Oof.*" He bent over double, and Jukes, giving in to his cruel nature, laughed out loud.

Chapter Twenty-Three

"Gold is hard, Jukesy," Jolly whimpered, holding his gut. "So, so hard."

Tiger Lily, still on her horse, wondered why this was happening. Was it really raining gold? Was Peter's old music box actually magic? At that moment, a chunk sailed past her face and smashed the empty jar she'd dropped to the ground. The mare stepped back, startled, and Tiger Lily struggled to stay on her.

"Whoa, whoa," she sang out, trying to calm her, but the mare kept reacting. She stepped awkwardly and high with her long legs, thoroughly spooked.

"Sorry," someone said from the shadows. Tiger Lily, pulling on the reins and cooing to the horse, looked toward the voice and saw Two, her shirt stuffed like a lumpy hammock, her arm thrown back, ready to pitch something.

"Wait a minute." Jukes picked up the object that had hurtled into his partner. "This ain't gold. This is just a rock! A regular ol' rock!"

Several more stones flew out of the bush, two hitting Jolly at once, one in the chest and one in the cheek. He went down hard, dropping his cutlass as he fell, knocked out for the moment.

"Enough!"

Jukes lifted his arm toward the sky and fired something—a flare gun. The sound brought the already scared mare up on her hind legs, throwing Tiger Lily from her mount. The horse galloped off into the woods, running from the chaos at top speed. Her rider had landed flat on her backside, all the air knocked out of her. She struggled to her hands and knees, willing her lungs to work. Hunched over, she could do nothing but watch as a pair of boots walked over and stood directly in front of her.

She looked up into Jukes's eyes. He smiled down at her. It was a smile full of malice and anger, so big she saw those black teeth again.

"Now, then, seems, thanks to the likes o' you, that we lost our fairy. But we got another prisoner instead."

She closed her eyes and waited for whatever would come next.

Chapter Twenty—Four

"*Ah! Ah!* Get away, you infernal pest!"

Tiger Lily opened her eyes to see little Sashi, newly freed and angrier than she'd ever seen her before. She was dive-bombing Bill Jukes, reaching for his eyes with her fingers, pulling at his greasy hair, kicking him in the ear with her feet.

"I said . . . get away!" He slapped at her, twisting his body this way and that to try to protect his face. The back of his hand connected with her little body, and she spiraled off, landing somewhere in the bushes.

"Sashi!" Tiger Lily gasped, listening for signs that her friend was okay.

"Well, cripes and crackers." Jukes righted himself, a

hand over his red ear. "Fairies is more dangerous than they looks. Should always be in jars, them."

"You monster," Tiger Lily screamed up at him, still panting with the effort to get up.

"No, I ain't no monster," he said, smiling. "Just a humble pirate, missus. And if I ain't getting the truth of a treasure outta you, then I'll take ye back to Hook. He'll squeeze it outta you, for sure."

At the mention of Hook, Tiger Lily's stomach lurched. "Hook? I thought you were on your own mission, alone."

"Oh," he said. "You've been spying, have you? Well, we was on our own, but it seems like you're gonna need extra convincing. Since we can't get the treasure our way, and we can't go back empty-handed and with no excuse for having been away, we'll just take ya back with us."

He nodded at his own plan as he spoke it. "That's right. We tell ol' Hook we was trying to bag him a captive, one that knows about a great treasure. That we managed to get her back to the *Roger* for him to interrogate, plank-style. Yeah, if we can't be rich, we'll be heroes at least."

"Wait." She struggled to her feet. "You can't take me out there. I'll . . . I'll tell."

Chapter Twenty-Four

Still holding his hurt ear, he looked at her with his head tilted to the side.

"Yeah, that's right. I'll tell Hook all about how you came here without his permission to find the treasure for yourself. How you were planning mutiny!"

There was a moment of near silence. Only the sound of waves crashing on the beach filled the air while the two adversaries stood face to face, their eyes locked and their chests heaving.

"You wouldn't."

She narrowed her eyes. "I would."

"He won't believe you."

"He doesn't have to believe *me*. He just has to doubt *you*."

Something on Bill Jukes's face told her he knew she was telling the truth. All it would take was one thing, one tiny thing, to set off Captain Hook. He loved making people walk the plank. It didn't seem to matter if they were regular people or his own pirates in the end. They all landed the same way—with a splash.

"Hey, Jukes," Jolly grumbled, having woken from his stupor, "I think the Andy thing is broken." He held out the music box, its lid handing from a broken hinge. Jukes clicked his tongue and shook his head.

"Put that blasted thing down. It ain't no Andon."

Tiger Lily took advantage of the distraction. She pulled her arms back, took a deep breath, and pushed Jukes square in the chest with all her might. Jukes was a tree of a man, but the shove caught him off guard, and he lost his footing. Tiger Lily didn't wait around; she didn't scream; she didn't keep fighting. Instead, she turned and ran as fast as she could, back toward the cover of trees.

There was a loud thwack as a knife lodged in a tree trunk, not far from Tiger Lily. She kept running.

"Argh!" Jukes screamed his disappointment when he saw that he had missed.

She could hear the blood rushing in her head. She had never been more scared in all her life.

"You'd best run, girl! 'Cause we ain't leavin' without you!"

When she heard the crash and snap of the pirates entering the woods behind her, she knew he was telling the truth. Still, she kept her eyes on the ground, searching for Sashi, as she rushed side to side, covering as much ground as she could.

"Lily!" Curly called to her from somewhere to her left. Then she stepped out from behind a large birch.

Tiger Lily was relieved to see her. That relief turned to joy when she saw Sashi, angrily pulling leaves out of her wings, perched on Curly's shoulder.

"Dang pirates," Sashi jingled. "Messing up my good wings."

Tiger Lily rushed toward them, and together they ran off.

Curly whistled long and sharp, calling the other Lost Boys to them. Free from debris now, Sashi took to the air.

"We're faster than them—we can outsmart them," Curly said, panting.

"They have my knife. And a sword," Tiger Lily answered.

"They gotta get up close to use those," Curly replied. "Best we keep far ahead."

Then she looked up and called out to Sashi. "You see the others?"

Sashi zipped this way and that. "Nibs is coming. But I don't see the twins anywhere."

"Shoot." Curly slowed down. "I'd better go back and check by the shore. Can't leave them out here."

"Wait," Tiger Lily called as Curly turned and ran back. "Don't go back there!"

Curly shrugged. "Gotta."

Tiger Lily checked for the pirates, who were far enough behind that she couldn't see them, but close enough that she heard them cursing. Then she followed Curly.

As she caught up, Curly said, "Lily, you should go. You're home free now. Get Sashi out of here."

"Lost Boys don't leave each other." Tiger Lily smiled; then they picked up speed, making sure to take odd turns and run on the rocks when they could. They weren't sure the pirates could track on land, but if they could, these steps would make it more difficult for them to follow.

Sashi swooped low and buzzed by Tiger Lily's ear. "Well, we always say we want adventures. Guess we should be careful what we ask for."

"Wow," Tiger Lily said. "You sound like my grandmother."

"Well, who do you think I heard it from?" Sashi replied.

Curly whistled once more, letting Nibs know they'd changed direction. This time, there was a short quick series of return whistles.

"The twins heard it, too," Curly said with a smile.

They were headed in the right direction. "Split up. We'll come at them from both directions, just in case they try to find us."

Tiger Lily nodded, and she and Sashi were off. It was quiet. No sounds of the Lost Boys anymore.

"I don't hear anything. Do you?" Sashi said.

Tiger Lily shook her head. "That's not good."

"I'll fly up and check."

"Stick close to the trees. I can't have you getting caught again," Tiger Lily insisted.

Sashi saluted, but she held the hem of her dress tight to keep the bells from tinkling. She could tease and joke all she wanted, but she had been shaken by her recent capture. "If I never see another jar again, it will be too soon," Sashi said. "I wonder if I could hollow out acorns to hold my jam instead."

After a few minutes, she flew back, out of breath.

"I saw them," Sashi said.

"Oh, good. They're all together? Are they headed back?"

Sashi was frantic. "They're together, but they're stuck. The pirates are close by. They can't leave without getting spotted!"

Tiger Lily thought. "Okay, we need a distraction.

Draw the pirates over here so they can make a run for it."

"Draw them over here . . ." Sashi's voice was shaky. "To us?"

Tiger Lily could see and hear that her friend was terrified—as she should be. After all, she'd heard the pirates talking about throwing her into the Neversea.

"Ah, no. Actually, Sashi, I have an important job for you. You need to do three things. First you have to sneak over to Curly and tell her to run as soon as the pirates leave—just run and don't look back. Then I need you to go get Nibs. And then the two of you need to get to the other side of the woods and find my grandmother's mare. She got spooked, but if I know her, she went back to the field. We'll need her."

Sashi put a finger into her mouth and chewed on her nail. "Are you sure? I don't want to leave you alone out here with those . . . men so close."

"I am positive," Tiger Lily assured her, trying to give her friend a way to get to safety without feeling bad about it. "I really need you to do this. You're the only one who can do it."

Sashi's chin quivered, and tears came to her eyes. "Lily, I have to tell you the truth." She took a deep breath. "I knew about the Andon all along. I just didn't want to tell you."

Tiger Lily was shocked. "Why?"

"Because you were acting different! We never chase treasure, nothing this big. We swim. We play. I just felt like . . . you were changing. And I"—she grew shy—"I don't want to lose you."

"Sashi, I would never leave you behind. No matter how much I change, I'm still me and you're still my best friend in the whole world." Tiger Lily wasn't mad—not even a little. She could understand the fairy's fear. She'd had it herself when it came to her growing-up decision. But it was not the time. "I love you. But you have to go, now."

Relieved and determined, Sashi swooped down, and the two friends embraced. It turned out it wasn't so hard to hug a fairy after all. And then she was off.

Tiger Lily released her breath slowly. Now she just needed to get to the shoreline and create a disturbance so that Jukes and Jolly would leave to investigate and the Lost Boys could make a getaway. She thought she knew just what to do. She rubbed her cheeks and then rubbed her hands together, trying to focus herself, trying to push away the worry that made thinking hard.

Then she made her way down to the spot where the pirates had set up their camp.

You've got this, Tiger Lily. You can do this. She tried to convince herself she was fine so she would feel like she was fine as she moved out of the trees and onto the open beach, where anyone could see her. In fact, she was hoping they would.

Chapter Twenty–Five

Tiger Lily planned to create a distraction that would lure the pirates back to the camp by the beach so that Curly and the twins could make a run for it. She hadn't thought much beyond that: making sure her friends were safe. But now that she was out in the open, she started to consider what would come next.

The wind picked up, and the trees began to sway. Each movement made her look; every sound made her jump. What was she going to do?

She looked for something heavy to throw. If she could make enough noise that they came out to see who was there, she might be able to dash back into the trees before they saw her. She just had to keep out of sight, keep quiet until the right moment.

She had just reached the spot where the pirates had dropped the music box when she saw the new arrivals: hundreds and hundreds of crows, crowding the sky, blocking out the sun, screaming and calling. Tiger Lily realized these must be the crows she had sent after her grandmother!

She sank with relief, knowing the Lost Boys would get away safely. But the crows had returned without her grandmother. She didn't know what to do. She could already see the pirates running toward the beach—toward her. She had no option but to run.

"Stop right there!" A knife whizzed just past her face and landed on the ground in front of her. She couldn't move fast enough, especially not on the sand. All that was left was to surrender. She was turning around slowly with her hands out at her sides when her toe hit something: the music box. And she had a new idea.

The pirates were just steps away. She took a deep breath, placed her hands on her hips, and stood tall.

"Stop right there," she commanded. And they did, but only out of surprise.

"What's this now? You're the one giving orders, are

ye?" Jukes laughed without humor. He was even more disheveled than usual and near out of breath. He had had it with all the chasing. "I don't think so, missus. This ends now."

"Yes, actually, I am giving the orders. I ordered you to come to me, and you did, didn't you?" She was getting better at this acting thing. She supposed being in mortal danger would do it.

"You did what?"

She spread out her arms, as if welcoming them. "I ordered you to the beach, and here you are."

"And how'd you do that?" Jolly was amazed.

"You fool, she did no such thing," Jukes yelled. "We came 'cause of the noise. We weren't ordered here or nothing."

"Oh, and I suppose I also didn't summon these birds," she said, pointing to the sky, where the crows circled. "This is just regular behavior, then? Random hordes of crows turning in the sky?"

Both men looked up. This? Well, this was a little harder to explain.

"So we're to believe you did this by yourself?" Jukes didn't sound scared, but he also didn't sound confident anymore.

"I did. With this." She pointed down at her feet. "The Andon. Turns out I *am* tall and brave enough to possess it."

Jolly took a step back. "I knew it was magic, I did!"

"You idiot. S'not magic. This is all a trick!" Jukes was angry, his whole body heaving. Spit flew from his mouth as he shouted. "And even if it were magic, it can't stop what's gonna happen now."

He grabbed Jolly's cutlass.

"Wait . . . stop!" Tiger Lily was backing away fast—too fast. She tripped over the uneven sand and fell, still looking at him, her hand held out.

"Oh, no, this is over!" he shouted, raising the cutlass high. And it was just at that moment that Old Crow dove from the sky and threw himself against the pirate's face, beak first.

"Ahhh!" Jukes dropped the cutlass, fighting to pull the bird off his face by tearing at his skin. "Get it off! Get it off!"

Jolly had lifted his knife and was trying to parry off the attacking bird. "I'm trying."

"Watch where you put that knife, you fool!" Jukes was frantic.

Then more crows screamed and dropped from the

sky, pecking and scratching and clawing at the pirates.

"It's her! It's the Andon!" Jolly cried out.

"Never mind. Get these fool birds offa me!" Jukes was staggering across the beach, covered in a swarm of black birds.

Jolly didn't know what to do. He was properly scared. He held out his empty hands to show Tiger Lily he meant her no harm. She just watched, too shocked to react.

"Don't send your birds after me. I'm leaving. . . ." He backed away, stopping to grab Jukes, still fending off the crows, and drag him down the beach to their boat. "We're leaving!"

The birds continued to aid her. Did that mean her grandmother had sent them ahead, and she was still on her way?

"Grandma!" she yelled. "Grandma, are you here?"

She turned this way and that, calling out for her grandmother to appear. But her voice was drowned out by the screams of both birds and men. Finally, the pirates were moving toward their boat, and any moment they'd be rowing out into the open water. The crows gave chase but stayed out of arm's length of them. Many returned to the sky.

Tiger Lily thought she heard a horse whinnying in the woods. "Mare, is that you?"

She started to head toward it.

"No one makes a fool out of old Bill Jukes!" someone shouted from behind her.

She looked toward the ocean, and there he was, running straight toward her at full speed, teeth bared, cutlass in hand again.

There was a high-pitched yell from behind her, and a long shadow fell across the beach. Pony jumped out of the bushes and ran directly in front of Tiger Lily, his head held proud, his muscles flexed and ready. And there, on his back, was her grandmother, with her braid flowing out like the woman in the cave painting.

It was as if her history had come to life and was protecting her from certain death. She sucked in her breath, her eyes huge.

Her grandmother sat tall in the saddle and glared out at the pirates.

"It's her," Jolly yelled. "The woman in Hook's stories!"

He picked up his rowing pace, and Jukes backed up into the ocean, trying to reach his partner.

"Wait! Wait, you fool," he spluttered, and splashed in the water.

But Jolly, terrified by the old woman on the white horse, kept on rowing. Jukes was forced to swim halfway back to Skull Rock before he finally caught up, splashing his big, clumsy body against the salty waves just like a bear.

When they were at a safe distance, Grandma dismounted and went to Tiger Lily, who still sat, in shock, in the sand.

"Are you okay, my girl?" Her grandmother got to her knees, pulled the girl to her, and held her against her chest. "Oh, I came as fast as I could. Good thing you sent those crows. Good thing Pony was back at home, too. He led me right to you."

A fast song played by bells alerted them to the arrival of Sashi. The Lost Boys weren't far behind. They saw Tiger Lily and her grandmother, saw that they were all right, and began to cheer and dance around, still yards down the beach.

Tiger Lily laughed, watching them, and her grandmother joined in.

"You've got some good friends there," her grandmother said, rubbing her granddaughter's back.

"Yes," Tiger Lily agreed. "I am the luckiest girl in the world."

Chapter Twenty—Six

When Tiger Lily woke up, it was already near midday meal. She opened her eyes, and the room was filled with muted light. The community had returned to the village a day early, and she heard their laughter and singing outside. She stretched, big and wide, filling her entire bed. She felt great, more well-rested than she had in days. The kidnapping, the witch journey, the chase—it had all caught up with her the previous night, and she had fallen asleep as soon as she lay down in her own bed. She had never been happier to fall into it.

She sat up, and her hand touched something folded and soft. She pulled a loose dress, all white buckskin and smooth sinew lacing, from the end of her mattress. Was this her grandmother's? Maybe she had left it there for Tiger Lily to wash for her. She held it up in the sunlight streaming in from the doorway. No, it looked clean. She pushed it against her face. It smelled clean, too. So she put it on. It was worn soft and fit nicely. She spun around in it and then hugged herself, enjoying the good feeling of the broken-in hide against her skin.

"I'll just borrow it, then," she said to herself.

She went to her wash area. Her wash basin was full and clear. Someone had brought in fresh water for her already. How nice. She cleaned up, washing her face and hands. Then she brushed her hair until it shone and pulled it back, tying it with a ribbon.

She was ready to start her day, even though it would be a late start. She wanted to get to Pony to take him out for a ride, to run with his wild friends, maybe. He deserved some fun. It had been a while since they'd just had fun together. But first she wanted to go visit with her grandmother. She had something important to tell her.

She crouched to get through the doorway and stood

for a moment in the full sun, enjoying the feeling of its growing warmth on her.

"We'll have to cut that door a bit bigger, I think," her mother said, laughing and turning a row of fish on a long stick over the fire. Tiger Lily had fallen asleep and woken up to the sound of that laugh for as long as she could remember. That was the kind of woman she wanted to be—full and loud.

Tiger Lily smiled back and turned to look at her door. "I don't know. It's always been fine."

She was a bit puzzled, but she had things to do. Maybe if she found her grandmother right away, she would stop back here to grab some fish before she went to get Pony. She kissed her mother on top of her head, told her she would be back soon, and left to find her Elder.

She didn't have far to go. Her grandmother lived just a few homes down, and she was out front working in her garden. Crossing the grass, Tiger Lily looked up and saw Gee, atop his own horse. She waved, but he didn't wave back. He just sat there, looking at her with a kind of shock, his mouth agape. She squinched up her face at him. What was his problem?

So strange, she thought, shrugging and walking on.

Tiger Lily, with no time to waste, walked to her grandmother and began to help her pull weeds.

"Grandma, I want to talk to you about the decision to grow up," she said. "I've been thinking about it, especially over the past few days. To stop those pirates, I had to make hard choices and come up with different plans. It was a lot of work, and I was scared at times—scared out of my mind, actually—but I did what had to be done anyway."

Her grandmother looked surprised at first, but she just listened, and a small smile grew on her face. Side by side they pulled weeds, with the younger one talking and the older one nodding now and then.

"I met a witch, LeeLee. Actually, I think she's your friend. She said you sing? Like that you can really sing. Oh, her rabbit wants to cook us dinner." She was speaking a mile a minute, not leaving any room for an answer. "But anyways, I've been thinking. I think I wore new pathways in my head," she said, chuckling.

"Pathways?" Her grandmother was puzzled, but the girl kept on talking.

"I know that growing older means more responsibility, but I also realize that it means more opportunity, more choices, more . . . life. And after seeing how much I could do to help my friends, I think I'm ready for a bigger life. I want to make my own clothes and go on overnight adventures on the other side of the island and maybe even learn to be a warrior, just like you."

She said the last bit in a lower voice. She was bashful and even confused. She hadn't known she was thinking it before she said it out loud.

"Well, of course you do," Grandma replied. Her tone told the girl there was nothing to be embarrassed about.

"Now, mind you, I'm not saying I'm making this decision for anyone other than myself," said Tiger Lily. "Because I would never do that. You taught me better than that. But I've learned so much recently, and, well, I know now that real friends are your friends no matter what—even if you get older. We need to change. Change is part of being human. And it doesn't have to be scary, and . . ."

She stopped. Her grandmother was laughing. Had she been laughing the whole time?

"What is so funny?" Tiger Lily asked, standing up straight.

Finally, the old woman settled down. She also straightened up, and cleared her throat, her hands held in front of her stomach. She looked at her granddaughter from her feet to her face. "I see you're wearing my dress, then."

Tiger Lily touched the garment, pulling it out from her sides. "Well, yes. I found it on my bed this morning. I thought maybe you left it for me to borrow?"

"And why, oh wise one, do you think I would do such a thing?"

Tiger Lily got embarrassed again. "Oh, you didn't want me to wear it? I just thought . . ."

"No, no." Her grandmother swatted playfully at her arm. "Of course I did. I wanted you to wear it. I left it because I knew you wouldn't fit your old clothes. I knew it as soon as I came inside your teepee with the wash water."

"My old clothes?" Tiger Lily was confused. "But I was just . . ."

The older woman held up a hand, cutting her short. "I think maybe you should go down to the sea. Take a look at yourself, eh?"

Tiger Lily touched her face self-consciously. Did she

have something on her? Dirt, maybe? She touched her hair. Was it sticking up?

"Just go, you," her grandmother said, patting her arm. "You're all right. Nothing's wrong. Just head to the water and take a good look."

Now she was really confused, but she did as she was told. She walked straight through the village. The people she passed smiled and called out to her. She wasn't used to this kind of attention and waved shyly. They even stopped and watched her pass.

Why were people staring? She walked faster, then broke into a run, her muscles limber and singing, her feet landing wide and solid. Boy, she was fast this morning. She covered the entire distance to the shore in half her normal time.

Huh, she thought. *Maybe I should sleep in more often.*

When she reached the shore, she was finally alone. It was mealtime, and all the children had been called back to eat. The men and women who crowded along the shore in the new day's early sun to wash their clothes and dishes were finished by then, and the area was deserted. She heard the peeping of frogs and a dove calling out to its mate. Nervous, she crept to the

edge, sat on a flat rock, and leaned over the still surface of the water.

Her reflection looked back up at her. Only, how
could this be her reflection? The face was definitely still
hers, but different. Her cheeks were more pronounced,
her jaw was more angular, and even her neck seemed
different. She held up both hands to her face, and
she saw them in the water, too, and they were different. Instead of looking at them in the reflection, she
pulled them in front of her eyes and turned them. She
gasped, reeling back from the edge.

"How?" she asked out loud. "How is this possible?"

Growing older wasn't supposed to be a surprise.
Even as she thought it, she knew that it wasn't a real
surprise—not really. She had been moving in this direction as soon as she began thinking about others first.

Her fingers were longer. She looked at her arms,
running her hands up each one, then pulled her tucked
legs out from underneath her and looked at them, too.
Finally, she peeked back at the Tiger Lily who regarded
her from the water.

She was older. She looked like a girl of about six-
teen. She had done it; she had aged. She had always

thought making this specific age jump from child-hood was something she needed to talk about with her grandmother, something that the Elders approved, that *they* made happen. But she had aged before she even started talking to her grandmother. She had just gone to bed one way and woken up another. Obviously, her body had already known her decision and started the process.

"Oh, my." She hung her head and giggled, imag-ining how ridiculous she must have been. There she was, telling her grandmother that she had made this big, life-changing decision, that she'd finally agreed to grow up—just a little—and meanwhile, she was stand-ing there, already grown! No wonder the woman had laughed.

In her heart, Tiger Lily knew how it had happened. By choosing others before herself, she had made her first grown-up decision.

That part was scary. She could make her own decisions—*had to* make her own decisions. But it was also exciting. She was in charge of herself. She would decide how she looked, how she behaved, who she became. The others—her family, her friends, her mentors—they would help inform those decisions, like they always did, but the decisions themselves would always be hers.

She stood up, tall, taller than she had been the day before, and looked out at the water, then turned to look back at her village. She felt bigger, and that was because there was a big feeling in her bones: pride. She was proud of what she had done and who she was becoming. And this was just the start.

Now that she was older, she could take better care of her village. She would spend more time with her grandmother. It would take more than a few new inches and lost baby fat to fill her dress.

Alongside the pride, she felt something else: a longing that made her eyes tear up, a new joy for all the possibilities of a life filled with choice. She decided right then and there that she would always value family, community, and herself. She would listen harder, work longer, and take the time to be grateful. This was the stuff of the best stories—decisions, chances, changes.

Suddenly, she understood what her grandmother meant, about wanting to know more, about wanting to see the new chapters as they were born, about wanting to hear as far to the end as she could. She'd already started it, and so far it had been one great adventure.

But first things first . . .

She found her friend by the water, cleaning a hunting knife. "Gee?"

He stood up suddenly at her voice, losing his balance and falling into the shallow water. "Uh, yeah. Hi, Lily. Wow . . . you look . . . different."

She laughed as he dragged himself out of the water. "Yeah, uh, I guess I kind of grew up."

"Yeah, kind of." He smiled shyly, nervously rubbing the back of his neck with his hand.

"I was wondering if you want to start training with me," she said.

"Training?"

"I want to learn how to protect the village better. I was hoping you and I could start spending afternoons with my grandmother," she suggested.

"So, learning how to wrestle bears?"

She laughed again. "Yes, learning how to wrestle bears, among other things." She got serious. "I just want to be more useful, for people to feel safe when I'm around. I thought maybe we could do it together."

Gee smiled at her. "I would love that."

They stood there for a moment, until it got awkward, and they started kicking the small rocks around their feet.

"Well, I'm going to go," Tiger Lily said, breaking the moment.

"Wait, where are you going?" He sounded a bit disappointed that she was leaving right away.

"I have to go check on a treasure."

"Treasure?" he asked. But she was already running off.

Tiger Lily found Sashi at the beach. She wasn't swimming; instead, she was sitting on the sand, watching the small waves rolling onto the shore.

"Whatcha thinking about?"

Sashi jumped. That was the second time Tiger Lily had snuck up on someone. She was pleased her new body remembered how to be stealthy.

"Oh!" Sashi flew up and around Tiger Lily, chiming sweet sounds and circling the girl. "You're older! Oh, I can't wait to put some designs on this dress. And we can make a whole new wardrobe!" She clapped excitedly.

Tiger Lily did her best curtsy, which was not very

graceful. "I am. I woke up, and, well, there I was, a bigger girl."

Sashi smiled wide, and then her smile faltered a bit. "I guess that means you won't be coming by every day."

"Why do you say that?"

The fairy sat back down on the beach and sighed. Even her wings drooped. "Because you're a grown-up, and everyone knows grown-ups don't play."

Tiger Lily folded her new height down until she was sitting beside her friend, both of them facing the Neversea.

"Tiger Lily?"

"Yes, Sashi?"

"I'm sorry I didn't tell you about the Andon." Sashi's voice was small, almost drowned out by the sound of the water. "I mean, I didn't know exactly about it—not what it really was. But when I thought it was a treasure and you might find it . . . I wondered, what if you loved it? What if you decided you wanted to be a pirate-fighting grown-up for real? What if that meant you didn't want to spend your days with me?"

Sashi's little shoulders shuddered a bit, like she was holding back tears. "But I guess it happened anyway."

"Sashi." Tiger Lily shifted a bit so she was facing her friend. "I'm not mad at you, but I am disappointed. How could you think I would ever not want to be with you?"

The fairy turned to her with hope in her eyes. "Really?"

"Really and truly. I'll have to take some hours to do new things. I'm starting to train more, and I'll be helping with different things around the village, but the days are so very long, and we have so much to do. I may be a young adult now, but I am still me. I will always be me, and if there's one thing I love to do, it's spend time with my friends, especially my best friend in the whole of the world."

Before she could say another word, Sashi had flown up in a flash and hugged her around the neck. Giggling, Tiger Lily fell on her back. After a moment, they stood and brushed the sand off their limbs.

"What should we do today, then?" Sashi was up and buzzing. "Swim? Climb trees? Check on Hook and the pirates?"

"How about we go see the Lost Boys? I think they deserve a good game of tag-you're-it for all their bravery yesterday, don't you?"

The two friends started up the beach toward the grass, where Pony was waiting for them.

"You know, Sashi, there is one big difference about me now," Tiger Lily said teasingly.

"Oh, yeah? What's that?"

Tiger Lily shouted over her shoulder, already taking off at a quick sprint. "I can finally beat you in a race!"

The wind was rushing by and her heart was beating loud in her ears as she ran, but she could still hear her little friend chiming behind her.

"Tiger Lily!"

She started laughing as Pony reared up on his hind legs and whinnied, cheering her on. It was going to be another great day full of friends and adventure. She really was the luckiest girl in the world.